Sex with Jesus

Mike Spiritfair Marty
Get a JAHB, LLC

Paperback ISBN: 979-8-9868943-0-0

Library of Congress Control Number: 2022916419
PHILOSOPHY / History & Surveys / Modern
EDUCATION / Philosophy, Theory & Social Aspects
DRAMA / Religious & Liturgical
SCIENCE / General

©2023 Mike Spiritfair Marty (Imprint)

Get a JAHB, LLC (Publisher)
Milwaukee, Wisconsin
USA

Dedicated to all of the crazy people ("crazy" in quotes)

The 48 underlined, italicized words in the e-book version correspond to the links for the 48 surveys at www.RealFair.org. (The novella price is approximately equivalent to 75 cents per survey for all of the 48 surveys.)

The print-on-demand version of this novella has the 48 link URLs for the 48 distinct online surveys printed in Appendix A. They are listed according to the *alphabetical* order of the book name links scattered throughout the novella (even though the 48 surveys were originally designed poetically according to a 1-48 *numerical* order). Whether the novella, or the group of online surveys, turns out to be the most important part of this composition is yet to be determined.

Dramatis Personae

Joebh
Noah
Haggai
Susanna
David
Jesus

Jehoshaphat
Al Wayne
Larry
Judge 1
Steven
Mike
Saul
Simeon
Some people
Prosecutor
Elijah
Granddaughters
Students
Teacher 2
Martha
Adult sons and daughters
Servants
Wife
Antiochus Epiphanes
Sons and kinsmen

Onias
Mary, the sister-in-law
Joakim
Judge 2
Kelli
Counselor X
Mary, the mom
John, the Baptist
Temple sellers
Peter
June Lynnae
Woman
Stephie
Teacher 3
Jasmine
Traveler
Smith
Mattathias
Army

Table of Contents

"Was ist dies?" Joebh demands.

"Joebh, we received an 'age discrimination in hiring' complaint yesterday," defiantly states Jehoshaphat, the VP of HR.

"Vehemently deny it in the response," Joebh articulates querulously, while working on a speech draft telling his employees how important they are. "There is no unfree discrimination. We choose who we want to pay to work for us, end of story. Why can't people understand that what happens is always just? There are no exceptions."

The CEO continues, "Everything is predetermined by chemistry and biology. There are no choices, I mean, we choose, but... I mean, there are choices, but, I mean, everything is just, because that's simply and undeniably how it is."

Lamenting, Joebh says, "I remember when whoever heard me spoke well of me, and those who saw me commended me, because I rescued the poor who cried for help, and the fatherless who had none to assist him. The man who was dying blessed me; I made the widow's heart sing. I put on righteousness as my clothing; justice was my robe and my turban. I was eyes to the blind and feet to the lame. I was a father to the needy.

"God is great. God is just. Life is good. When we realize how vast and beautiful the creation is, we are learning about the Creator at the same time, for He is the Creator of beauty. How beautiful is the bright, clear sky above us! What a glorious sight it is!"

"Yes, but be careful," Onias, the former High Priest in Jerusalem, interjects, "for as Isaiah 45:9, Isaiah 64:8, and Romans 9:21 suggest, God fashions the Earth's matter, but

God is not the original instigator of the elemental materials that are found in the sky and all around us. For instance, let's say your dick erection is 7.75" long and 5" in circumference. This would be a gift, or consequence, of nature, not a gift from God, the YAH-way. God and nature are not synonyms. There is a possibility--not yet determined--that God is a subset of nature. Is God only the brain working, or is God more than this?"

Onias continues and says, "The poor will never cease out of the land; therefore, you shall open wide your hand to your brother, to the needy, and to the poor in the land. You shall follow what is altogether just, that you may live close to God. Have you heard about Jesus?"

"Yes," the CEO moans. "Mental health is being able to deflect, or to overcome, others' subtle attacks, but we still haven't figured out the best strategy to deal with his annoying, dominant proclamations. Some of them are joths, but... Turn the other cheek? Confess? Don't defend? That's ridiculous. Life is war, the war of living. As Clausewitz says, everything, and everyone, contributes to the war effort. Formerly, war was expensive, but now we produce baby customers to supply any future depleted ranks of soldiers. Adults who don't produce any baby customers, and who don't add to the pool of possible future soldiers, aren't doing their part."

"Yes, that's the capitalistic spin, but is the data compatible? Your attitude is proud and arrogant," Onias persists. "The Word of the LORD is the Word of the truth. The Word of the LORD is something that rings true for people from all walks of life--flying or falling, crying or crawling. When the _word_ quits its widely-accepted, truthful ringing, it stops being the Word of the LORD, even if the pragmatists would like to keep calling something true that isn't."

"It's a little chilly," Joebh remarks. "I should probably joth. I will not argue with your accusation. In the past I gladly shared my morsels of food with the orphans. But now I say, It is vain to serve God. What gain is it to obey the YAH-way and to mourn for our sins? I try to be decent and kind to the workers, even though I probably think of them a little bit too much as machining slaves."

Onias goes on, "Blamelessness consists of our public confession and in listening for correction and guidance. The gain is peace and righteousness, weapons fashioned into _plowshares_."

CHAPTER TWO

Al Wayne, the pipeline financial engineer from Babylon, says to Noah, "The _idols_ Succoth Benoth, Plutus, and _Bel_ motivate me and help me not to be _lazy_ like _Mary_, you know, Martha's sister."

From his posh listening perch, Noah affirms, "Okay. So, then, why are you here?"

"My optimism bias sometimes puts people off, particularly for those whom I care about," Al Wayne states. "Is suicide mental illness or is suicide unhappiness? Obviously, the data say it's unhappiness, due to the way a person's involvements in the world have progressed, some of which are the way they have been treated by other people over the years."

"I disagree with those statements. You're free to be false, I suppose. I do agree that it's a challenge for people who want to die to relate with people who don't," Noah sums up. "Thurstone's laws of comparative judgment are always in play. And, essentially, various places of worship are mostly designed to keep unhappy, but productive, people sufficiently confused so they won't be able to think clearly enough to choose suicide. Sometimes, however, it doesn't work. The Mental Health Act of 1959 is an example of dealing with market failure in this regard. Believe it, or not, sometimes we have to keep people alive against their will."

Al Wayne conjectures, "Is that loving, or is that the opposite of love? Would a _lawyer_, and the law, allow that?"

"I'll find out," Noah says when he ends the session and reads and eats the oblong vitamins and minerals joth sitting on his desk: The Lord is one. Love the Lord your God with all your heart and with all your soul and with all your mind and with all your strength.

In the back luxury kitchen, Noah cooks a frozen glop to perfection for lunch while he prepares for his afternoon showdown with Larry, who mentions a recurring cube[1] dream. "If you sin and succeed, the approach of death will be unappealing because of the enjoyment of living on the shallow fringe. That's side one. Then, God is available to help when you are in need. Okay? Side three--if you do good and confess, the fear of death is defeated. Then, If you sin and don't confess, your life will have more than the usual allotment of troubles. Side five goes something like this: If you sin and fail, death will hold more allure. And last, it said people generally receive less punishment in life than they deserve. I don't know about that. So what does it mean, do you think?"

"Hmm, sounds too explicit and definite to be real," Noah hedges. "I'll give it some thought. Larry, it's legal to keep people of sound mind alive, right, if they don't want to be alive, even if they justifiably will feel _robbed_ and manipulated? As an attorney, what's your take?"

Larry replies, "Certainly, the legality depends on the age of the people and on their levels of productivity. I wonder if calling suicide a mental health problem is a way of deflecting blame away from those who are still living and onto each helpless, dead person who can offer no rebuttal. Maybe Mental Health Day should be called God Day."

---

[1] https://youtu.be/JPKfkDH6Lgw

The teacher, _Haggai_, asks the government to _lend_ him some money in the form of <u>student loans</u>[2], but, because of _righteousness_ and age discrimination, none of Joebh's private-industry companies subsequently hire him. "_Loosen_ the bonds of wickedness," Haggai shrills sullenly, as he picks up a spherical fission joth and hurls it down the enclosed ramp. "My qualifications exceed your needs, but your efficient ways and goals are gruesome. They exemplify how snugly and smugly applicants are able to fit into the make-believe culture of ends and beginnings. No references from four smug ones? No hire! Yes, make! believe? You must make (yourself pretend to) believe what you do not believe; no one can believe what he believes is false... though he can pretend he does. But what does the data say?"

As he serves the LORD by sitting in a pew the next Sunday morning, Haggai hears the talker drone on about <u>St. Matthew 23:8-9</u>[3]. When the Plato-ridiculed hour for the LORD concludes, the people intone, "World without end, amen, amen. Ejaculation and making babies without end, amen, amen. World without end, amen, amen." The talker says to Haggai when he exits the service area, "I am glad to be your father in the LORD. How are you?"

Haggai responds and says, "I am purposefully unassimilated and rationally suicidal. How unkind of you to ask." On his way out, he wonders, Is making babies ad infinitum the only way to live? The invisible kingdom of God is what Plato describes at the end of the ninth book of the

---

[2] https://www.youtube.com/watch?v=NNS7KL3AjxM
[3] https://www.bible.com/bible/114/MAT.23.8-9.NKJV

dialogue[4]. Hegel twists the invisible kingdom of God into an abstract human-race organism which is accomplished through infinite ejaculation. Verses 4:3 and 7:14 of Daniel describe the everlasting kingdom that lives through the generations. So, what does Daniel mean, and has Hegel's twist of the infinite kingdom become a kingdom of good for the whole human race, or has it become a kingdom of terror that is desired by only a small minority of human beings?

Haggai tries to get rid of the student loans that he has been unable to remit from his school salary discretionary income. Judge David reviews his claim and dismisses it.

This trigger unhinges Haggai's mouth: "I'm weary of working hard on my thirteen joth scripts to no avail, in a similar way that most of the exploited and oppressed peoples of the earth are, even though I am aware that over 80% of purported educational expenditure outlays for students go to teachers' salaries, like mine. I'm weary of those who care about the happiness of the economy and who lie about the YAH-way. I'm weary that the way of the naturally selfish prospers and that idols still have not been _eliminated_. I'm weary of those who proclaim false peace and who make the moneyless money slaves feel worthless. Capitalism is a pack of thieves continually siphoning funds from every possible nook, crack, cranny, crevice, and corner."

---

[4] *The Republic*

CHAPTER FOUR

Joakim's attractive OB-GYN doctor wife, Susanna, goes into the garden of the courtyard over her noon hour for a rest and a bath, but two of the court's judges who _perpetually_ lust for her independently sneak in beforehand.

One of the men hurries toward her and says, "The gates are locked and no one will see us." He slides his hand under one of her arms.

Then the other judge appears and tries to coerce her by saying, "If you refuse, we both will go to court and swear that we saw you send your servants away so that you could be alone with a young man."

Susanna's stunning breasts visibly heave from the stressful situation. Through her forming tears, she looks up to the sky, but she resists crying out for help.

Instead, the 34-year-old doctor states forcefully: "Pause and wonder. Why do you do such things? Men of understanding, as the YAH-way lives, and as your soul lives, will there not be peace and truth? Everyone who is born is caught in the web of sin. There is no one in the present generation who has not sinned. Yet from days of old, from that time even until now, men live by the fruit of their conduct and actions. They are joined one to another; they stick together and cannot be parted. Remember this, a lying tongue hates those who are crushed by it. If it be so, our God's occasion to test me, while this is being done by your hands, I will strip and go naked."

The two men stop.

She continues in her high-range tone: "The YAH-way in his holy knowledge knows full well that I could escape from you, yet I can gladly suffer with joy in my soul because of my devotion to the Jewish God. I came naked from my mother's womb, and I shall have nothing when I die. YAH-way gives and the YAH-way takes. Blessed be God the Fashioner. Hear Thou from heaven, Thy dwelling place, and forgive. Deal with each person according to the confession of his conduct, for You alone see and know all the acts, facts, and intentions of men, while we mortals are left to operate in weak, strong, and semi-strong reservoirs of information."

One of the judges walks back and forth, thoroughly bewildered. The other sits down astonished.

Susanna says to them, "Rest and be still. You both must have crept through the narrow gate to the garden. My joth this morning reads, Strive to enter through the narrow gate... If the proverbial 'broad gate' means wanting to have enjoyment and pleasure with experienced women, maybe the narrow gate means striving for procreation with unskilled maidens. God is giving, but women... women... often can't be. Women have to be careful and smart. Anyway, I have two kids and I have a broad gate, not a maiden's gate. Whether broad or narrow, striving should never be sneaking, because lusting is the opposite of loving. May the YAH-way deal kindly with you."

The first man stops pacing and says, "Susanna, you are righteous, more than we knew. And now, O our God, what shall we say after this?"

Both men leave the garden.

Susanna exhales and whispers, "I have escaped by the skin of my teeth. God's availability in the time of need is beyond fathoming. God gives _generously_ and graciously to all. How I wish that someone would help us to remember these _important_ words by recording them in a <u>book</u>[5]!"

When she leaves the garden, she passes Steven, a lawyer whom she knows. She overhears Steven arguing at an

---

[5] *Just Another Holy Book*, M. S. Marty, Get a JAHB, LLC

abortion murder case, as he says, "Adultery is a stoning offense, and no less so is the taking of life by abortionists. The burden mothers must bear is a loving gesture in order to raise the little up-and-coming workers who will fuel the growth of the economy, for the economy's benefit."

Susanna's first appointment after lunch is with Kelli and Mike. "Good day," she says. "Give me a minute, and I'll be ready."

Kelli and Mike nod their approval.

"Your neck is like an _ivory_ tower, your eyes like the pools in Heshbon. Your nose is perfect beauty. Behold, you are fair, my friend. You have dove's eyes. How beautiful are your feet in sandals, the curves of your _thighs_ are like jewels. Make haste, my erotically-charged _honeybuns_. Be like a gazelle...," Kelli, the native from _Cherokee_ reads quietly from a book[6].

"Okay, what brings you in today?" Susanna interjects.

Mike suggests, "We're weighing an abortion at this point."

"I see. Would you like to tell me any of your reasoning?"

Kelli looks at Mike circumspectly and says, "Babies are kind of correlated with death. Sex and procreation move Earth's beings from point A to point B in time, generationally, but Mike, and I, are still a little unconvinced that this endeavor is something in which we would like to participate."

"Yes, that's good," Susanna agrees. "The Belmont Report says OB-GYNs should be respecters of persons which, interestingly enough, is the opposite of what we are often taught about God... who is not a respecter of persons. Yes, the autonomy of each patient's right of choice, based on the availability of options, is paramount."

"The pre- and post-slavery of the mom has to be balanced against the need for new servile workers to be born into the

---

[6] _Just Another Holy Book_, M. S. Marty, Get a JAHB, LLC

economy," Susanna goes on. "Sometimes people say kids are a gift of God, but is the data compatible? Genital size, in fact, is a combined effort of nature, reason, and hereditary planning. No Christian verses, and only Psalm 127:3, mention children as a gift of Hashem--that's a pretty vague phrase that must be consolidated with all of the other surrounding factors. Abortion kills children, or it kills potential children. If you really love each other, and if you love yourselves, it's maybe best to have an abortion, but if you love the economy of the investors, having a kid might be a sacrifice you would be willing to make."

As Mike and Kelli leave, Susanna reflects for a few seconds and then again reads the joth snack sitting on the corner of her desk before she chews it slowly and swallows.

CHAPTER FIVE

In Joakim's court, Judge David presides over a case in which Saul is charged with insurrection.

Saul offers to take an oath, and David responds: "Yes, you may, though I do not require it. The mouth is a small part of the body, but it makes great boasts. Consider what a great forest is set on fire by a small spark. The mouth also is a fire, a world of evil among the parts of the body. When we put bits into the mouths of _horses_ to make them obey us, we can turn the whole animal. Since perjury is so rarely adjudicated, we are stuck in a stump where the best liars have an advantage, any oaths cause additional _strife_, and they don't really help streamline the proceedings. Opposing counsel will try to impeach your falsehoods if you resort to them, but you're free to be false... unfortunately. This is what the data say."

David grabs the circular, knobbly joth from the robotic conveyor in his chambers, and he glances at the caption: Do true.

David meets with Noah and another counselor, and Noah asks, "Judge, how are you doing? Why do you look so worried today?"

David replies, "I was at rest in my house, and these were the visions of my head while on my bed. It is God who has dismayed me. Behold, I go forward but He is not there, and backward, but I cannot perceive Him. Should He come near me, I see Him not; should He pass by, I am not aware of Him. Am I brain-damaged?"

Noah thinks then says, "Hick's law details how the time it takes a person to make a decision is a result of the possible choices he or she has. Increasing the number of choices increases the decision time logarithmically. Have you been thinking too much about your cases, or about something else? There are an infinite number of possibilities in thinking, and, even though there is a significant correlation between IQ and human information processing speeds, infinite possibilities can derail the best of us. I won't even start in on information-theoretic entropy, or SIS."

The other counselor says, "Most importantly, has it been affecting your caseload? Damage to the brain is the root cause of less than 5% of mental health worriments. You're being awfully emotional about this. It's not normal... for you, I mean."

"Yeah, it's nothing," David mumbles. "The woman botheration. I guess it's my childish conscience besetting me. I think women are a criminal activity. Sell it all, give a bit, sell a bit. Being celibate maybe is best. Is there a conscience of fun? Women like to have fun, don't they?"

"Fun can be an escape," the other counselor proposes. "It can also be a form of delusionalfulness. Sometimes fun is the opposite of loving, in regards to loving women, I mean. Is it criminal to be with a woman? It is not necessarily for everyone, at least I don't think so. It is an unsolved problem, however, even if your worldview is Hegelian, which is the predominant worldview, whether acknowledged, or perceived, or not. I guess Kant and Hegel both reinforce the deus ex machina finite/infinite connecting mechanism plot device that the theologians are embedding, and people often refer to their guardian angel, but that is only a pragmatic allowance."

deus ex machina   * sex w/ Me

Noah avers to his co-counselor, "I'm not certain to what you are referring, but what David is saying about celibacy makes me think of Bowditch's all-or-none law: the magnitude of a nerve or muscle response is unrelated to the strength of the stimulus--all that matters is whether the response threshold stimulus magnitude has been met; if not, there is no response. In other words, it's all or nothing."

Interceding, David adds, "The phrase 'rule of thumb' comes from Bradley v. State of Mississippi, which stipulates that a man can only beat his wife with a 'rod not thicker than his thumb.' The Mississippi Supreme Court voiced approval of the husband's role as disciplinarian and stated its belief that the law should not disturb that role:

> Let the husband be permitted to exercise the right of moderate chastisement, in cases of great emergency, and use salutary restraints in every case of misbehaviour, without being subjected to vexatious prosecutions, resulting in the mutual discredit and shame of all parties concerned.

Is it okay for husbands to hit their wives with switches smaller than the width of a thumb?"

Noah says, "No, but... publications estimate that one out of every three marriages has spousal violence. On the other hand, psychological or emotional abuse is not usually treated as a criminal offense, partly because of the difficulty of investigating and proving such abuse."

Noah continues, "Some people have a conscience of justice. Some people choose to have a conscience of truth. Emotion-regulation knowledge helps various types of people to regulate their emotions to serve the goals of their predominant trait, either pro-social or Machiavellian. Dr. Jekyll's Hyde hides; maybe he is aware of his shadow traits, or maybe he isn't. If aware, Machiavellian Hyde hides, while pro-social Hyde hides... less."

"Am I Machiavellian? Maybe," David acknowledges.

CHAPTER SIX

Since, in more ways than one, unrighteousness is necessitated for a man and a woman to make a connection, deus ex machina, God directly impregnates young Mary of Bethlehem, who gives birth to a child. She says to Simeon, a friend, "He shall be called _Jesus_."

The adult Jesus becomes a minister in the _land_ of Judea. He makes an appointment with Noah, and Jesus begins clarifying his thinking when he asks, "What should I do about John the Baptist who is baptizing at Aenon near Salim? His _reputation_ is significant, but I do not necessarily agree that everything he says is strictly true."

"The things that bother you about what he says, do they fit the data? Say more," Noah begs.

"John says he saw the Spirit dive as a dove out of the heavens upon me. What? Really? He also says God is able to fabricate human babies out of rocks. I'm also not sure that soldiers should be content with their wages. Incidentally, is my deus ex machina a co-creative world fabrication?

"When someone says to me, How are you?, I would like to exclaim, 'I am in the throes of childbirth,' or 'Every step is filled with pain.' What is man? Of what use is he? The good that he does--the evil that he does--what does it all mean?" Jesus pleads. "Will the upright and blameless be seen as upright and blameless? Will the kind be treated kindly? Will those having integrity motivate integrity in others? Will the merciful be shown _mercy_? Will life be crooked for those who are twisted? Aristotle says the matching principle applies to one's habits."

"Uh, valid musings," Noah agrees. "As Wilder shows in the law of initial values, the response of any bodily function depends to a great extent on what the starting point (stasis) is. Let me mention a <u>cube</u>[7] dream someone described to me recently. The patient gave me permission to anonymously share it."

Thereafter, Jesus speaks to some people, and he says, "If anyone thirsts, let him come to Me and drink. He who believes in Me, as the scripture has said, out of his heart will flow _rivers_ of living water. A fountain shall flow from the kingdom of God. And everyone will live wherever the river goes, because the water flows from the sanctuary. Take hold of the river and don't let go. Then you will discover the peace of mind she offers, and she will become your joy. Whoever hears My words and yet does not follow them, he or she does not know Me intimately. Most assuredly, I say to you, if anyone keeps My word, he or she shall never see death."

And he continues, saying, "God is kind. He or she who is not kind does not know God. Animal sex with women means the world will keep going, but it will stay the same, or it will become worse, and there will be death, always death. And there will be slavery of feelings, and there will be torment and discontinuation pain, spasms, a lack of liberty, i.e. slavery, and there will be... money."

He goes on and says, "Loving money is the opposite of loving Me. Money is a part of animal sex with women, but money does not have to be a part of sex with Me. There are different ways of having, hoarding, earning, making, stealing, losing, using, and abusing money, and most of the ways are traumatic. Some ways are more righteous than others, but many of the ways are inexcusable. Serving the world instead of serving Me is insanity, a waste of time and effort."

---

[7] https://youtu.be/JPKfkDH6Lgw

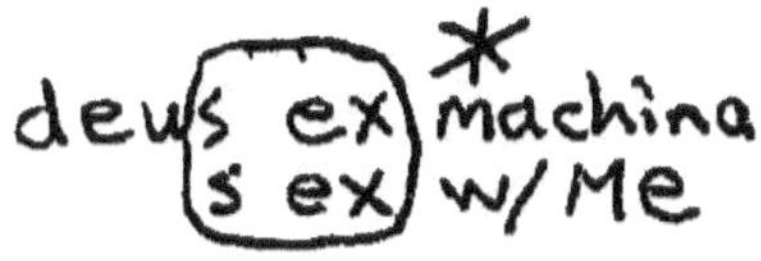

"Sex with Me moves the world better, not worse," Jesus resumes. "Blessed are those who separate the mind from the body, and discrete and detached are those who have intercourse with Me instead of with the genitals, for only these mindful separatists can improve Earth's relations. In the kingdom of the LORD, there the wicked cease from troubling, and there the weary are at rest. There the prisoners rest together; they do not hear the voice of the oppressor. For those who identify with their genital size, both the small and the great are there, and the servant is free from his master. Blessed is he who is not _offended_ because of Me, blessed are those who have been persecuted for the sake of righteousness, and blessed are those who have been persecuted for the betterment of humanity."

Back at his home, he looks at the rectangular joth on his desk: Come to Me, all you who labor and are heavy laden...

CHAPTER SEVEN

Is schizophrenia a gap between the mind and the body (physical reality) or is it a gap between <u>what someone says</u> and <u>what someone does</u>?, Jesus ponders in his journal as he grabs a comestible joth from the slider, reads it, eats it, and continues his ruminating. Hypocrisy is only a small subset of lying and unrighteousness, he writes. I have to remember Marty's <u>Scant Alignment</u>[8] and Euthydemus:

> O Ctesippus, I think that we must allow the strangers to use language in their own way, and not quarrel with them about words, but be thankful for what they give us. If they know how to destroy men in such a way as to make good and sensible men out of bad and foolish ones--whether this is a discovery of their own, or whether they have learned from some one else this new sort of death and destruction which enables them to get rid of a bad man and turn him into a good one... I offer my old person to Dionysodorus; he may put me into the pot... kill me, boil me, if he will only make me good.

Jesus continues writing: Noah says schizophrenics are split in two when the mind's infinite creativity cannot be contained within a person's finite body, when he or she is not anchored sufficiently within the mundane physical reality, and when his or her thinking isn't more-or-less able to integrate into the human body's limits. I see it, however, as unintegrated metaphysical alignment and fragmentation within that same mundane physical reality.

---

[8] https://youtu.be/cTEJsV6iBL4

He speaks to a small crowd that has gathered near the sea, and he says, "A new commandment I give to you, that you help one another with _lovingkindness_, as I have loved you."

And he says, "Parts of the world are fabrications of nature by God--good--working through us, but other parts of the world are fabrications of the devil--da evil. If you--your body and your mind--are happy in the world, it might be the good parts of the world that make you happy, or it might be the evil parts of the world that make you happy, or else it might be some parts of both. If you are happy, you have no reason to make changes to the parts of the world that keep you entertained and pleased. The pre-established harmony between the infinite mind and the natural body is tight, but unhappy people choose to see a world that would allow them to be happier within that vision--their kingdom of God. People whose minds or bodies are not pleased with the parts of the world that surround them are the people who need to have the courage and faith to push for better worlds, better ideas, better happiness. Some people need to kill parts of themselves and be reborn with new life, similar to how Socrates describes his mission of being a midwife to the birth of new ideas. Some people's minds dictate actions of the lower sort, toward da evil, self-serving money and sex targets.

"Public confession is the cornerstone of the greater kingdom, while when confession is a secretive thing, a hidable secret, done only in secret, confession becomes the opposite of confession. When confession is lying, it itself becomes the cornerstone of a faith that is a false facade for fakes."

Concluding, he says, "If you concentrate on the satisfaction of your own interests, future worlds will disintegrate, because these are the goals of evil, but if you do good, through your actions, and you reinvigorate future worlds through your goals of good, you will have less trouble--and more peace--in the land of the living; death, and the approach of death, will be defeated by your exemplary kindness and by your confession. This is what the data indicate."

Jesus goes on and says, "Religion too often is a pragmatic, 'rule of thumb' enterprise that gets vaguer and vaguest as time rolls on, because both the people and the priests cannot but speciously believe what they do not understand.

"The scriptures explain how God the Fashioner interacts with those who are merciful, integrated, kind, and upright, but for those who have selfish, not universal, intents--for those who are pragmatic and twisted, for the close-knit families and tribes--life will be crooked, not straight.

"There are also the people of the land, the gaia people, who want to keep the earth populated for the devil's purposes, the people who try to be universal by being caring and passionate about saving Earth's dirt, water, and air. Yes, they want cleaner air... for themselves and for their children after two or three billion poor people have--thank god--died off. Save the Dirt! Infinite Dirt! Lauds to the Dirt!

"Many reformers will manipulate what is true and turn it into what is false--Is God merciful randomly, or reasonably? Reasonably, most assuredly, I say unto you. If you understand these words, you shall have no terror from the death of your body. In fact, you do not really exist. Even I do not exist, because my life on Earth is finite."

Jesus goes into the temple and drives out all those who have been buying and selling in the temple, and he overturns the tables of the *moneychangers* and the seats of those who are selling doves, and he says, "I believe I am mentally solid, I am not in denial, and I am not deluded. And how are you? The scriptures declare, 'My Temple is a place of prayer; but you have turned it into a den of thieves.'"

Jesus is arrested, and he tells his captors: "I am finite. So are you. You do not exist. See you in Sheol."

June Lynnae, Susanna, Joakim, and David watch as Jesus stands in Joakim's court, and the prosecutor says, "Are you the King of the Jews?"

Answering, Jesus says, "You say correctly that I am a king. For this I have been born, and for this I am alive, to bear witness to the truth."

And Jesus continues, saying, "Animal sex moves us from one place in time to its subsequent place, little by little, day by day, year by year, generation after generation. Listening to Me is like having sex with Me, and by so doing we will move from this time to a future and better time for all of Earth's relations. Do not worry, but seek the kingdom, and unravel the present world so a new world can begin."

During the trial, a bystander confronts one of Jesus' disciples, Peter, who is looking out of place and _suspicious_. Peter denies being one of Jesus' disciples.

CHAPTER EIGHT

In Joakim's court, David presides over a case in which the Federal Trade Commission determines marketing that suggests tomatoes are _vegetables_, rather than fruits, is not substantively misleading for the purposes of nutritional information.

The prosecutor calls Elijah to be a witness in the proceeding with regard to the _intent_ of the advertiser and the nutritional _nourishment_ value of tomatoes.

Since Susanna does not have any current OB-GYN appointments, she is a bystander in her husband's court.

"We all make mistakes," David digresses. "Yet as Dante says, 'On either side it pours; On this devolv'd with power to take away Remembrance of offence, on that to bring Remembrance back of every good deed done... both of which must first Be tasted ere it work; the last exceeding All flavours else. Albeit thy thirst may now Be well contented...'

"I drink too much beer; I confess. Once, when I was young, I shamefully ate showbread from the temple; I confess. I like listening to the music of harps, I do so whenever I can, I like praising God with loud _instruments_, and I've tried to learn the harp myself. Music is an indulgence of mine; I confess."

"You are an _inspiration_," Susanna snidely remarks to David when the trial recesses for the day, "although music often is used as a way to deaden God the Fashioner's influence and _establish_ pragmatic public policy patterns."

Elijah knows Susanna through her mother, June Lynnae, so he stops and listens as he makes his way out of court.

Susanna asks the judge, "Do you believe in the God of the living?"

"I do," David replies abruptly.

Susanna barks back, "But does it fit the data?"

"As I said," David goes on, "we all have needs, some more than others. We all make mistakes, but God is gracious and punishes each of us less than we deserve."

"Then is God not just, or does justice not relate to punishment? Do you hear a voice, or do you ignore it, it only being a troublesome _insult_? As the scriptures say, Do not My words do good to him who walks uprightly?" Susanna questions confrontationally.

Ignoring Susanna's questions, David's 7-incher goes on, saying, "God fabricates the world according to his wishes."

Interjecting, Elijah says, "Contrarily, Judge, some parts of the world are fabricated out of nature and are God good, while other parts of the world, also fabricated out of nature, are evil. Things grow; that is nature. Sometimes good thinking allows noble thoughts to come into our heads; that is God. God and nature are not identical. Pragmatists intentionally imply that they are because it benefits them to say so, but God only fabricates the good parts. God is helpful and generous and good; da evil devil isn't.

"Not without exceptions, but, generally, the people who talk the most about religious things are those who are the least religious, the least interested in religious things. A person can either talk or do. Talking is the opposite of doing. People who talk like to give the impression of their devotion so they don't have to do the cumbersome actions such devotion would reasonably require.

"Likewise, generally, the people who talk the most about integrity are those who have the least integrity, understand the least what integrity means, and have lives that are the least integrated. Again, a person can either talk or do. Talking is the opposite of doing. People who talk like to give the impression of their integrity so they don't have to examine and perform the cumbersome actions of which an integrated life would reasonably consist.

"As JAHB-V 3:12 states, Everyone who does evil hates the light, and will not come into the light for fear that his deeds will be exposed. But whoever lives by the truth comes into the light, so that it may be seen plainly that what he has done has been done through God."

David thinks twice, then he says, "It sounds like Jesus is influencing you, but universal benevolence is not a Jewish requirement. The state takes care of these matters. We submit and live accordingly. I have to go. I should joth."

"And further," Elijah continues before David escapes, "saying that a finite human body has an infinite, eternal, everlasting soul, and then denying Descartes' mind-body duality, essentially says that the exact same thing is both correct and incorrect. Explain the mechanism or apparatus that connects a finite body to an everlasting soul. No one can. There is no such mechanism. There is no soul, per se, except to the extent that soul means direction or vector. The eyes are the window to the soul--the entrance, sensors, and direction of our seeing--which influence the direction of our thinking. The direction of our thinking influences the direction of our choices. The composite pre-established harmony of our brain thinking, and of our eye viewing, influences the future direction of our friends, of our families, of our companies, of our nations, of our alliances, of our planet, and of our universe.

"As Jesus says, having sex with him is the closest thing to an interaction between finite and infinite things. We still don't quite fathom it. Hegel, of course, tries to merge finite human beings into an infinite organism through deus ex machina. Is everyone still caught in the web of sin, or not? Still caught, it seems."

As David leaves, he whispers to God, "Dante says, 'the world is twisted... By a bad head.' If only one didn't have to sin to connect with a woman, but nature makes it so. Indeed, I am the one who has done very wickedly, but I like having sex. What am I supposed to do? You are generous, but women aren't. Your gentleness and patience have made me great. You are **a guard and an angel**. No wait, was it the priest, or maybe the counselor, who said that last week? 'A guard and an angel' or 'a guardian angel'? Homilies should come with subtitles."

CHAPTER NINE

June Lynnae vents when Susanna tells her about the event in the garden. "They don't care about anyone but themselves. They're narcissists. You shut them up; that's great. I could just pinch their arms off for wanting to make you a sex slave. Any financial recourse for yourself or for the climate?"

"The _LORD_ protected me," Susanna says, "no harm was done, and I got to experience a divine rush. All in all, I could just let it go, or I could repay evil with good. You know, sometimes I harass Joakim with nagging, too. It's not the same. It's maybe not as bad. Maybe it's worse. As Marcus Aurelius says, "When thou art offended at any man's fault, forthwith turn to thyself and reflect in what like manner thou dost err thyself..." and,

> [B]e of a benevolent disposition towards him, and if, as opportunity offers, thou gently admonishest him and calmly correctest his errors at the very time when he is trying to do thee harm, saying, Not so, my child: we are constituted by nature for something else: I shall certainly not be injured, but thou art injuring thyself, my child.—And show him with gentle tact and by general principles that this is so, and that even bees do not do as he does, nor any animals which are formed by nature to be gregarious. And thou must do this neither with any double meaning nor in the way of reproach, but affectionately and without any rancour in thy soul; and not as if thou wert lecturing him, nor yet that any bystander may admire...

"We are part of one another, but who are 'we'? Where do we draw the line, spatially, time-wise, gender-wise, political-wise, creed-wise, species-wise? If we adhere to self-interested, tribal mentality, is that a necessity, or is it due to intentional political propaganda to get people to waste energy attacking each other? Is God able to influence our gene somatic mutations through our reflections and behaviors? I hear Jesus calls us co-workers and co-fabricators with God the Father. Maybe God the Father is in our thoughts, God the Mother is nature, and God the Son is the resulting created thesis-antithesis-synthesis outcome of each event in which we partake. Maybe fathers can raise children but then should soon after become brothers to them. Do you have the munchies? I could joth."

"Don't be a coward," June Lynnae tells her. "Elijah told me that courage is a tonic for melancholy."

Susanna continues expressing herself by saying, "I'm not melancholy. Are you? And I don't think I'm a coward. What does God want? As Rank says, sex is a disappointing answer to life's riddle, but both these men must have some feelings of terror they are trying to avert. Well, there's something for them to think about... not according to their expectations, obviously. Angry recompense does not help righteously. For what is my life, your life? It is even a vapor that appears for a very little time and then vanishes away. I came from you naked, and I shall have nothing when I die."

June Lynnae retorts, "My life will fade away, your life will fade away, and, as you say, you can't take it with you, but can you keep it with your Jewish DNA?"

"Joakim is wealthy," Susanna continues, "and your two granddaughters won't be socio-economically commonplace. I'm not unhappy. Are you? Often I cringe at how clannish we Jews are. Sometimes we Jews are hated for being so. Do we have a good defense for not being hated, or is being hated entirely reasonable? Do we reflect and consider, or do we just ultimately ignore the barbs? If we want to live in ways that are hateful, we have no justifiable right to complain when we are legitimately maligned."

"Uhh...," June Lynnae is stymied, and sputters.

Continuing, Susanna says, "In sexually-reproducing organisms, children are infinity modules that diversify the human race to guard against extinction in fast-changing, unpredictable environments. The personal genetic recipe of each partner is diluted by half with each offspring. This helps ensure there will likely be offspring produced who happen to have the right DNA code to survive. If we don't procreate, when we die, does our DNA die... off? Our DNA? My DNA? Your DNA? Jewish DNA, what's that? If you procreate, you don't die, you get diluted, infinitely diluted/deluded. We are diluted deluded to think that hereditability is like immortality and that we live on through our kids.

"Each woman and each man have germ cells--one strip of DNA--and soma cells--two strips of DNA--that are almost identical except for a few variations that make people different from each other. The DNA strips of humans and chimpanzees are 98% identical. If we look at base pairs, the difference between men and women would be about 1.8%. Two men, standing next to each other--regardless of class, race, or creed--have DNA that is well over 99.9% the same. Ergo, it's a stretch to think kids and grandkids and great grandkids pass on 'your' DNA through the generations. It's more like each kid passes on 'human' DNA immortally, or until we humans are extinguished someday.

"Visible characteristics, or phenotypes, and their convoluted underlying genotypes, can be either dominant or recessive (Aa or aa). The different versions are called alleles, and they each specify the kinds of proteins that are created uninterruptedly. Each individual is also like a dominant or recessive gene; either one or the other. Most human behavioral traits have some basis in the genes we each have been given. Traits don't dilute over generations, but you do, unless you are your traits. Even if you identify yourself with your traits, these traits would also dilute unless they are all dominant. If you primarily identify with your genital traits, these germy germ cells, with their constitutional DNA, also dilute when each zygote is formed.

"We inherit 37 mitochondrial genes only from our mothers, which helps us watch maternal lineage. These gene sequences sometimes partially seep into the nuclei. A woman passes on her egg DNA to her children. A man's nuclear Y-chromosome, with around a hundred genes, is virtually identical to his father's, and so on, and we can track paternal lineage this way. The DNA in our other 22 pairs of nuclear chromosomes, called autosomes, get reshuffled, not just in each generation, but in each child. Gene expression varies over time, as either mutations or as polymorphisms. Each human newborn averages about 60 new mutations. Any single gene usually has only a small influence on phenotypes. So, am I really my dominant gene traits? Is that who I am?"

"Nonsense. I'll see you in a fortnight, dear," June Lynnae says, as she gives her lucent daughter a real, regardful hug.

CHAPTER TEN

"And certainly not least," Haggai begins where he left off, "I'm weary of women. Sex is violent. Sex ≠ pax. Love is peace. Sex is the opposite of peace. I guess, sex and making babies are part of the war effort. 'Make love, not war' is a tricky slogan that really means 'make war, make war.' Everyone who is born is caught in the web of sin primarily because it is a sin to be with a woman, physically and metaphysically. It starts with sin because violence is a sin. There is still no avenue for sinless sex with women. Only liars say that men who don't have sex with women are homosexuals. What a misinforming laugh. There are a thousand other reasons--some self-chosen and some extrinsic. Sex with women is not metaphysically aligned with anything... except with Hegel, and with war, and with violence. People with unintegrated metaphysical alignment are not seeking the kingdom, and they want to join the capitalistic den of thieves. I wonder if Danny Joseph had any girl troubles that led to his teenage suicide on April 7th? Is what Jesus says accurate: There is no terror from the death of one's body? Did Elijah fearlessly walk into a tornado as a free man after his altercation in Joakim's court because he believed his reasonable time on Earth had ended?"

"Hey, guy," Haggai hears a woman call to him. "How are you? Could you help me get something to eat?"

Haggai shakes his head regrettably. "I don't have any cash with me," his intentional choice walking to the grocery store to buy some basics with a debit card. "On September 2nd, I had an 18-year-old willing woman on my bed, but I said no, and on June 24th, I watched a movie about Frida Kahlo with a 19-year-old woman. Both events were wrapped in secrecy, both events were normal and natural, but normal and natural are many times a frightening mix of sickening, bestial, malappropriate, unsanctified thoughts and acts."

She says, "Ooh, why are you still talking to me? You're not any use. Get away from me."

He gratefully complies, as he thinks, It sure would be nice to be dead so I wouldn't have to face my Scientific Methods' monsters tomorrow.

Back at home, in his artistic bubble, his public sinning and confession of conscience channel reaches a cumulative 400 million views.

The new school day starts and he bears the expected reproaches and scornful laughter from the students. He gets a bumpy joth capsule and looks up at the cylinders on his screen. Why don't these joths hardly ever match up with those joths?, he wonders as he drops it in the tunnel.

Polytheism is the belief in many gods, but there is one god only, the original Jewish God that meets the human spirit inwardly, the One, Living, Inward, Spiritual God of Reason, Mutual Experience, Written Record, and Sensitive Awareness, Haggai contemplates while his students work on an activity. People and genders differ on what is reasonable and rational. This is a problem, but this is monotheism. The polytheistic historical cultures are Roman, Greek, Norsk, and Egyptian.

German and Anglo-Saxon pagans are the normal people of the land. Paganism is different from pantheism, which says that God is everything, that everything is God, and that God has a plan. Most happy people are pantheists. Jesus isn't one of those, though Paul, his replacement, might well be. Pantheists are akin to naturalists, who generally believe that everything is as it should be (think Pangloss); God approves of everything that happens and believes in the wonderfulness of the status quo. Examples are Berkeley, who was Bishop of Cloyne, Leibniz, and the Jewish Machiavellian relativists,

Einstein, with his ten relativity equations, and Spinoza, though Spinoza is difficult to classify and is maybe a panentheist. Various idiosyncratic, speculative people are often in the panentheistic group, including people who identify with emotions and feelings rather than with the thought and reason of God. Reason fabricates nature into the world that we have. Jesus talks about the wonderfulness of God the Fashioner but not about the wonderfulness of the status quo.

Satanism is self-interest and semitism is clan-, or Klan-, interest. Machiavellianism is personal reputation consciousness with a focus on outward appearances. Machiavellianism tends toward "whatever you can get away with." Conversely, Christianism is universal-interest. Christianism is thinking, but it isn't magical thinking.

How can a thing cause itself into existence? Isn't that what existentialism is? Won't my parents resent me for doing what I want instead of doing what they presume? If you have to sin to connect with a woman, and it's a sin not to connect with a woman--who wants to have sex with me, anyone, anyone?--then sinlessness is not really possible, but public confession of sins is. Public confession generally neutralizes sins' unrighteousness. "Okay, hand in your sheets. Next we will talk about Goodness of Fit in regression analysis."

On the bus home, Haggai writes, Sin 1: tense relationships. How can this be changed? With the fabrication of a new resentless world without the necessity of the baggage that comes with relationships (but not lost or floating). Sin 2: feeling meaningless, miserable, and invisible. How can this be changed? By resentlessly understanding, and living with, God. As Aristotle says, God is the self-motion of thought which is the opposite of loneliness (miserableness and invisibility). Sin 3: inferiority complex. How can this be changed? By resentlessly understanding the creatureliness, and false boasting, of everyone, including the greats. Sin 4: eggless ejaculation. How can this be changed? With courageous, resentless public confession, as <u>Marty</u>[9] shows. Self-actualization overcomes all resentment.

Back at his apartment, Haggai opens the door when he hears a knock, and he says, "Hey, what's up?"

Three of his fellow teachers enter, and Stephie says, "How are you?"

Haggai responds, "How do you do?"

Stephie speaks and says, "We've been worried about you. You spend a lot of solitary time in your own little bubble. Do you ever think about harming yourself?"

Haggai thinks and states, "Certainly, but not lately."

"Why, when there are so many good things in your life, and there are also the people who care about you?" Stephie goes on.

In reply, Haggai says, "I've tried to have sedulous resolve in attainment with some of my extracurricular artistic risky counter-cultural efforts, and that's helped. The wayward slave rumors bug me, of course. My student loans, and my failure to break into the private sector in my career, still irk me. But mostly, it's Ed Cowdrick and the gospel of consumption experiment that was fueled in part by Ed Bernays. These two atheistical Eds wanted to turn workers into consumers in order to make even more money off of them than could be accomplished with them as factors of production. Bernays' Jewish mom, Anna, Jewish dad, Ely, and Jewish aunt, Minna, are sister, brother-in-law, and sister-in-law to the Jewish atheist, Sigmund Freud, and Minna might also have been Freud's secret co-whore cohort. It's debatable.

"It's the whole 'everyone is my enemy' human tendency. Hardin, with his Tragedy of the Commons, was from Dallas, which is the center of global contrived content. The counterreform movement has a large network of law schools, institutes, and think tanks that pour out an endless stream of this worldly crap. Movies and music play a part. Non-profit foundations, even, will be happy to approve any money requests as long as you do exactly what they want to have done anyway--you just end up providing the free manpower. More inequality is good for innovation--is it? Hardship is good for poor people like me--it is? Government is bad--is it? And rich people's capital taxes should be relatively small--oh, really? That's contrived content creation.

"But... I'm trying to learn to avoid the sin of being judgmental along with my other sins. It's not easy, but it's moderately important, I think."

CHAPTER ELEVEN

Martha asks Noah, "Having sex with your Mega Monster is great, of course, but is something bothering you?"

"We've had a great life, but death is peeking at me a little too eagerly. If I am my own king, and if you are my lady, why... Ortega writes that he who was never lost never gets to successfully grapple with his own mortality. My mortality. It's just something I've been thinking about. If life is bigger than me, why should that peeve me? Jesus is history, did you hear that? There's a furphy that one of the prosecutors' wives protested against charging him. But, as you know, Martha, she might have really not liked him, and wanted him to be charged, and expected him to be charged, but she, as a woman, tried to deflect blame away from herself by feigning her protest.

"I even wouldn't be surprised if someday marketers and money-grubbing theologians figure out a way to get billions of people to mindlessly praise the execution of the poor Man of the People, even if mindfully, consciously, they should realize they're being scammed."

"Meaning what?" Martha prompts. "Shallow shalom. Aren't you you? You're pragmatic, Jewish, resourceful, talented. This is who you are. Don't think too much. You should be happy, even as your existence gets closer to ceasing."

"I wonder what my life would have been like without you?" he rudely asks.

Martha stares and says, "You don't mean that. You should apologize."

"I'm not apologizing," Noah states. "I'm just thinking out loud. I'm just doing what I want by owning my thoughts. I'm not doing anything wrong.

"The law of effect doesn't really distinguish between outcomes that are based on decision-making thought processes rather than on instinct, or on sensory information storage. Mill and Bentham, of course, made this distinction. Or, I guess, Mill did; Bentham didn't. Clearly, it's possible to die without thinking about it. That's what you recommend?"

Martha continues: "I wonder if Emmert's law relates at all to the approach of death... the perceived size of an object changes as its perceived distance away does."

Noah responds, "Yeah, that sounds like a stretch. Anyway, I think I'm beginning my downward slope. Mental arousal is important for productivity and performance, as Yerkes and Dodson delineate, but a superabundance of it at this point might be anti-productive, I'm afraid."

"Okay, and?" Martha bolsters.

"I heard someone mention recently the interesting observation that Israel and "is real" sound the same. What Israel? Are we really moving through space at 360 miles per second? It doesn't feel like it to me. Maybe it did to the guys who wrote, Stop the World--I Want to Get Off. Then again, maybe they meant the less-tangible, cat-and-mouse, head-spinning, whirled world rather than the more-tangible, physical dirt Earth.

"It would be nice if we could perceive What Israel. Was ist dies?--the noumenon, the unknowable 'thing-in-itself,' as Kant says. Is there objective reality truth? It's a strange question to ask, but it really should be asked... often. Am I just a liar to my patients when we talk about a reason for living? In perception, how does quantum entanglement interrelate with the Gestalt laws that show that all people do not even see three-dimensional objects in the same way when their DNA, memories, and interpretations of former perceptions, differ?

"Similarly, Bloch's law always mystifies me; how does the duration of a flash of light--ophthalmology--relate to psychology? If the eyes are the window to the soul, as some say, I guess what you see is where you go, the direction of your life. And the longer you see it, the brighter it becomes--'seeing' the light, 'seeing' the kingdom of God.

"Maybe there's a subtle, tremendous, yawning rift in meaning between **believing <u>in</u> God** and **believing God**. I think most of my transferable skills relate to me loving me, or to me loving us, and, even though many of the skills are thought processes, they are different from the thought process that synopsizes **believing God**."

"You mentioned DNA. What does that have to do with this?" Martha asks.

"A lot... maybe," Noah answers, as he casually picks up and snarfs a joth from the conveyor. "Epigenetics, methylation, and hereditability provide some clues about how our behaviors are correlated to our individual genotypes and phenotypes. And, as I was saying just a bit ago, there might be a fairly robust contrast between different types of people and what they each reflect in their thought pavilions, or God, or the LORD. Some people reflect good thought pavilions, while others have a more repetitive, heuristic, pragmatic, self-interested, small-minded, short-sighted, lying, cheating, stealing, atheistic, biological, Machiavellian, emotionally-intelligent thought pavilion... which might... be me... or you. As Bloch's law indicates, it makes a big difference.

"Both atheistic and good thought pavilions are very similar in terms of capacity and potential. It's the goals and the contents within the thought pavilions that differ. What happens in people's thought pavilions also relates to Fechner's, Weber's, Stevens', and Herrnstein's laws, which all expose how the size of a just-noticeable stimulus can vary greatly in effect between a calm thought pavilion and a chaotic thought pavilion. Socrates describes this in his description of casks and colanders. Perhaps it means whether we think like a human or have INSTINCT like an animal. Even autism or dementia could possibly relate to epigenetics in the sense that a medical insult, so called, causes damage to a tissue, causes damage to an organ, or causes a DNA mutation. I don't know. Maybe if we treated psychological and emotional abuse more as a serious criminal issue, there'd be less dementia. Can our environment and interactions--insults--cause DNA mutations? Certainly it is a possibility. In a sense, the thought pavilion is the God orifice, almost like having sex with God, without utilizing the genital orifices, of course."

Martha ends by saying, "Yes, dear, just promise me you won't recommend Mary. I know she hasn't had a child yet, but she still supports the economy with her occasional, outrageous spending forays."

"Don't worry," Noah assures her. "I won't. This one dream a patient described still miffs me. It indicates people are punished less than they deserve. Would that be unjust? Is life? Is getting away with whatever one can get away with in life a sustainable metaphysical system? I guess it is, if one can get away with it. Even if people can, though, maybe someday our goals will be more aligned with less spurious metaphysical strivings; less greed, less crime, less sin, more lucidity--sounds dreamy... someday."

Noah continues thinking and says to himself, Is an overstimulated life reasonable? Can it be?

When he talks with Martha's sister, Mary, Noah says, "I think much of your depression relates to your realism. Yes, penetration means mental acuteness, being able to penetrate the intentionally-designed falsehoods in the world, but you see life even a little too realistically, which can be overwhelming and cause dysfunction. Should I suggest you be more delusional? Uhh, that, however, would not be the standard treatment. Mental health is alignment with the LORD, serving the LORD. The LORD is the prevailing cultural spin direction, with its underlying, hidden goals... which are revealed only on a 'need to know' basis. Nevertheless, there are many alternative, possible directions: bad directions, good directions, etc., which is why mental health is such an undiscussable public topic, and which is why we try to constrain these discussions to the therapeutic office."

"And what if someone refuses selling herself or himself to the official incentivized direction?" Mary conjures. "If the LORD God is direction, is spirit, and if each little person joins in uncomplainingly, good for each of them, but happy is the heroic one who is aligned and united with her own unflinching direction. I think pragmatists operate better in chaos than in a straight line. Certainly, believing God the Fashioner and God the Friend is not REALLY something you can say, it is only something you can do."

Noah replies, "You might be right. What would you need to <u>do</u> to be heroic to yourself, for a yaşama sebebi, in order to find a place in civilized society?"

A short pause later, Mary, operating at full-potential strength, asks Noah, who is floored, "Does your civilized career consist of doing enough things to make you feel heroic?"

"Uh, uh... This is your session, not mine," flounders Noah, as he starts to write out Mary's committal papers.

CHAPTER TWELVE

Joebh takes a skytrip rollercoaster and arrives at the top, unmanned floor of the giant, Tarpan rectangular-stick joth hub, one of 472 scattered outposts on the earth, 335 of which are sea-based and completely submerged. Inside each outpost, the two top-floor cylindrical tubes, typically viewed virtually, or not viewed at all, contain the Jurisdiction of the Hungry and the Jurisdiction of the Homeless joth statues, each in its own tube. Joebh quickly makes the obligatory obeisance, picks up a round joth pellet, and slips it into his pocket for later.

A slanting-down, circular marquee, like a long polymer, double-helix molecule, wraps the Hungry statue cylinder and parades these six jigglers in a loop:

- Love YAH-way, the one God, with all of your heart, mind, soul, and strength;
- The gate leading to life is narrow: choose it;
- Learn from My gentle heart so that your spirit will find peace;
- Instead of worrying about your earthly needs, seek the righteousness of God's kingdom. When you do, YAH-way will provide for your needs;
- Desire the treasures of God; earthly treasures can be stolen, but not the treasures of heaven;
- Realize you in the infinite universe.

Likewise, the Homeless statue marquee displays these six jigglers:

- Do good to those who hate you and pray for those who mistreat you;
- Call YAH-way your father and no one else;
- Do true;

- Show unselfish kindness to your neighbors;
- Do not judge others unless you are perfect... and you're not;
- Behave toward other people as you would like for them to behave toward you.

He enters a secret panel behind the statues, closes the panel behind him, and treads down a short flight of stairs. He receives a conductance and abruptly stops.

Jasmine, the _messenger_, had ridden by _Gethsemane_ at the Mount of Olives on a flying rotocopter all the way to _Uz_, and electronically delivers the message to Joebh that his Jerusalem tenement, where several of his adult sons and daughters are staying on vacation, has collapsed in a blaze of unknown origin. The children have been killed, along with a _traveler_ and a few servants, including Smith, the man who trims several of Joebh's lawns.

Joebh cries out with pain in his flesh, "Why, oh, why? This _touches_ every fiber of my being. Do I deserve such evil? Am I _greedy_? Do I pervert justice? A bribe blinds the eyes of the wise and _twists_ the words of the righteous. Do I show partiality or take bribes? I am _confused_. Am I the most ignorant of men? Where is the YAH-way? I am filled with pain as though something were relentlessly gnawing at my bones."

Joebh calls Onias, who challenges him, "Your feasting is the sin of gluttony while others around you hunger."

Eventually, Joebh hangs up and resumes his trek downwards, as he peaks his nose through around a dozen different levels of the structure, making sure the two million Tarpan hungry and homeless people are verifiably still alive, slaving away like good little feeble boys and girls. Feeble though they are, the two million jam-packed sardines in each joth hub are a pragmatic necessity, after the robosourcing of past occupations, and to keep the consumption of energy and other resources viable for the rest.

On the trip back to his office in the skytrip rollercoaster, he looks at the joth from his pocket which reads, Whatever you wish that men would do to you, do so to them.

On the office phone, Joebh tells Onias, "As you know, I am the administrator of all the jothing operations."

"Yes, I know that," Onias states.

"The Jurisdiction of the Homeless statue goads us into living, and reminds us that when each of us dies, we, too, will be homeless," Joebh goes on.

"Yes, and to remind us what benevolence is, and what its opposite is," Onias tacks on.

"Also, the Jurisdiction of the Hungry statue reminds us to be thankful for our well-oiled nutritional supply chain," Joebh asserts.

To which Onias says, "It keeps us mindful of both bodily hungers, and of the pain and destructiveness of letting them roll on naturally wild."

"Anytime anyone wants, people can visit the observation level of their closest joth station," Joebh tells Onias pedantically. "Normally, people just receive their heating and eating joths and view the statues virtually, on occasion. Onias, can you tell me why the Jerusalem tragedies occurred, given that I am such a good person?"

"I'm afraid your wealth has deceived you and made you willingly blinded," Onias says. "For affliction does not come from the dust, nor does trouble spring from the ground; yet man is born to trouble, as the sparks fly upward."

"Teach me, and I will hold my tongue," Joebh tells Onias. "Show me how I have erred. If I am wicked, woe to me."

"I have a message from a priest of the Jehoiarib family named Mattathias, from Modein," Onias goes on. "A document indicates that you are related and that both their families and yours have common ancestors. If you come and help them, then they will come and help you at the time when you cry for help."

"What is the help that they need?" Joebh enquires.

Onias tells him, "The wicked ruler Antiochus Epiphanes, son of King Antiochus the Third, sent a large army against the towns of Judea. Then he launched a fierce attack and issued a decree that all the people should abandon their own customs, adopt the official pagan religion, and offer sacrifices to idols. But Mattathias answered in a loud voice: 'Although all the Gentiles in the king's realm obey him, yet I and my sons and my kinsmen will keep to the covenant of our fathers.'"

"Hmmm, I will think about it," Joebh declares unconcernedly.

"Do you believe that you are related?" Onias pushes. "Are all humans related to each other? Or are you a near-sighted biological atomist who, on purpose, fails to admit the noumenon? DNA and genes are helpful facts, but the real view is still obscured. Only pragmatists say you will go to heaven when you die, which is not true. The Germans, Kant, Leibniz, and Hegel, promulgate the religion of Familianity and the passage of 'going to heaven,' but what is true is that when you die, your measly, momentary individual existence will end.

"Do you think your existence is different from Mattathias' existence? Do you think that his essence and being is separate and distinct from yours? Do you think that your genes are everlasting, that your genes are the determination of your life's trajectory, that people with a handful of distinct genotypes from yours are the cause of their separation from your life, and that genes and biology are the natural cause of everything pleasant for you in your middle little life? Maybe genes are more like genies and jinni than we want to admit

48

and maybe evolution is a form of creativeness to which we are invited to help shape.

"Every once in a while, mutations occur in mitochondrial DNA that signify distinct haplotypes. Can we prove that genetic mutations, mitochondrial or nuclear--a single guanine replaced with an adenine, for example--are accidental? Does natural mean accidental? Does accidental mean natural? Does accidental mean random mean natural? Does thinking cause DNA mutations? Can thinking mutate a peptide? Is thinking natural or abnormal? Do only schizophrenic realists really think?

"The human race is like a sexually-reproducing organism. Sex and babies in the human race are like meiosis cell replication for the gametes, the sex cells. 'Sex Sells,' as we have heard many times. Schizophrenic realism thinking, on the other hand, is like mitosis cell replication that could cause mutations to help heal the human race from its ills."

In the towns of Judea, soldiers attack Mattathias and his kinsmen. The Jews do nothing to resist. They do not even throw stones or block the entrances to the caves where they are hiding. They proclaim, "We will all die with a clear conscience. Let heaven and Earth bear witness that we are being slaughtered unjustly, that every Jewish family of every future generation in every province and in every city should remember this day for all time to come."

Joebh replies to Onias' relay about the killing spree and says, "Clear conscience? So what? What's that?; nothing but a pragmatic delusion. As Epictetus says, The door is always open."

Joebh then meditates speculatively, One possible reason for people not to kill themselves, or a reason to live, is that sometimes it is said that felos-de-se will cause pain and suffering for family or friends. It makes more sense to me, however, if it doesn't mean the subsequent suffering of family or friends, but more generally the subsequent suffering of certain people on Earth. Perfect justice is difficult to establish on Earth, partly because it's so difficult to define in a mutually-agreeable way. The fact that there is injustice--some who have more than they 'deserve' and some who have less than they 'deserve'--is not completely surprising, as Ecclesiastes states. If, perchance, those people who think about committing suicide think they are unhappy because they have less than they deserve, if they end up committing suicide, the result will be that other people will possibly find themselves now having less happiness than they deserve while previously they had exactly what they felt they deserved or more than they deserved. Since, on a planet where justice is difficult to establish, generally, truthfully, there will probably always be those who feel they have less than they deserve, as well as those who might be willing to admit that they have more happiness, etc. than they deserve. Felos-de-se, therefore, cause more suffering for others, even if arguably less suffering for themselves, and it is not necessarily the most 'honorable' path, unless of course one believes as a principle that everyone should commit suicide and he or she is trying to set a precedent.

I suppose a person who commits suicide is like a company shutting down a business operation whose revenue is greater than its variable costs, even if it looks like the operation is running at a loss once the fixed costs have been allocated. If the contribution margin is greater than zero, shutting down the operation will transfer the fixed costs that need to be allocated to the remaining operations, whose profits will all then be diminished. In this case, some will possibly find themselves now running at a loss when previously they were able to accrue profits. I wonder if living human beings often resent successful felos-de-se.

Joebh's wife calls. Without showing deference to her interest, Joebh starts up his rant again, "Hello, darling. Organisms molt cells. The human race molts people. And we are supposed to keep producing babies for God and for the economy... infinitely. The common, sanctioned, and accepted delusion is that people who have kids sustain their personal, individual existence through these kids, but the further we go back in time, the more diluted are our connections with any individual people... and the more our set of ancestors becomes similar to everyone else's. Individual succession of individual human beings--human being cell-people in the human-race organism--is mostly fiction and fantasy because it doesn't withstand the facts very well. Do you suppose women or men are more deluded, generally, with regard to this out-of-sight, out-of-mind, he who has ears to hear, unwelcome upshot? Did losing our kids in Jerusalem make you, or me, more distraught than logically necessary? I am finite. So are you. In essence, in time, we do not exist. That Israel."

Joebh hangs up and asks Jehoshaphat, "Machiavellians, atheist Jews, and Satanists EXPECT others to lie, cheat, steal, hate, scam, and plunder against them, but is this what they WISH would be done to them, or not?"

"I think operating in this atmosphere is their perceived strength," Jehoshaphat candidly states, "so, yes, I think this is what they both expect and wish to be done to them. Here's a point I noticed from the discrimination complaint Haggai filed: Do people's potentials conflict with those of others? In other words, if one reaches one's potential, does that squeeze out others from reaching theirs? If so, to what degree?"

Jehoshaphat continues, "As with all humans, you, and the business council, believe that injustice is better for you than justice, but justice, perfect justice, is the way of peace, real peace."

Joebh says, "Yeah, I guess that fits the data."

Thinking about his own tragedies, and about those of Mattathias' cluster, Joebh calls Onias and says, "I've been thinking about Marty's banned YouTube letter[10]. Do you know which one I mean?"

"Sure," Onias tells Joebh.

"Did you know slaves are important to capitalists, indispensable even?" Joebh asks.

"What are you saying?" Onias comments.

"I am for peace, but when I speak, They are for war, the business council, I mean," Joebh relates. "I guess, business and life are part of the overall war effort. Real reveal, shall I?... What Israel?... The joths obscure the real view. The joths are just talking--signs--posters. Can I lie if I don't wish others to lie to me? The joths allow us to hide the slaves we keep alive against their will through suicide prevention--all of the unhappy people who would prefer to be dead... not necessarily molted, but just dead. Since it is best not to molt them, shed them, by taking them behind the shed to be shot, we outpost them. This is the best alternative. Workers used to be customers, and then they became consumers, but then too many of them started consuming too much. Now we hide them at the joth outposts and transpose them into machines that consume the minimum of inputs, and, like a machine, they don't technically need a home, just a fitting place in the machine gears. Jesus is the one rambunctious person the business council couldn't justify 'keeping alive.' Being a good, docile, productive slave was not something to which he was amenable. Amen?"

Joebh goes on, "The joths around the cylinders aren't always the same as the eating and heating joths because of the diversity of versions and translations. Are the joths bad?

---

[10] Appendix D

Are they an idealistic facade? Do they encourage people to believe a lie?"

Onias thinks and says, "What you believe is not what you sing or say. WHAT YOU DO IS WHAT YOU BELIEVE. For example, people, even some Jews, often like to append the adjective Christian to themselves, or to natural events, or to other things in which they are involved. Like the joths, adding an adjective is saying something. People often, maybe always, say they're Christians, not because they are, but because 'Christian' sounds better, generally, than saying you're an atheist, a pagan, or a Satanist. But what you do is what you believe, not what you say. Awkwardly, with pre-established harmony and matching, in business and in life, when all the buffers have been removed for the sake of efficiency, so the billionaires can steal an extra $60 billion this quarter, there is no wiggle room left to be ethical, by moving toward justice, if one prefers, and MRP nervousness eventually creates an unstable, unsustainable system. God enters the world through our goals and steps. Good enters the world through our goals and steps. Infinite goodness enters the world through our goals and steps. An atheist believes in money. A Godder believes in good. An atheist loves money. A Godder loves good. Havers of money are haters of good. Loving money is the opposite of loving good."

"Do scientists want to move toward justice, or just ignore justice?" Onias piquantly asks. "Do Godders want to move toward justice, or ignore it? Do democrats want to move toward justice, or just say they do? Do republicans want to move toward justice, or ignore it? Do women want to move toward justice, or ignore it? Do men want to move toward justice, or just say it? Do you have the potential to be just? To answer your question, I guess the joths are only a lie until... they become REAL."

Joebh thoughtfully says, "Thanks, Onias, bye," as he hangs up.

Onias whispers to himself, "Not the world's jurisdiction, nor the pleasures of the broad-gate, a third thing--what do I want?--to make the joths real. Maybe that's Joebh's job."

Picking it up from the corner of his desk, Joebh reads the skytrip rollercoaster joth again, then he drops it down the chute.

Dramatis Personae Details

Joebh

Is a CEO. Has a wife and several sons and daughters. Works at blamelessness by publicly confessing and listening for corrections from God through his mind. Visibly resents the palpable annoyances of Haggai. Confuses nature and God. Is not aware of many of his existential defects, such as gluttony. Has bad breath during an episode of gnawing pain. Has an individual family, biological mindset.

Noah

Is a psychologist. Does not have integrity, but works hard to maintain an appearance and reputation of integrity. Has at least 400 important skills in his repository. Is successful without any major resentments. Has a biological mindset.

Haggai

Is a teacher. Bears insults from others, including from his students, and sometimes resents people who laugh at him with scorn and who try to shame him. Is often sullen and otherworldly. Has many existential defects that have not been overcome. Discusses righteousness and the public confession of conscience with others when he can. Reprehends idols. Has always sympathized with the downtrodden. Feels weary that successful people are often wicked. Is put off when disingenuous people talk about hope or peace. Believes authorities frequently lie about the YAH-way. Is aware that the words evil and good don't have canonical definitions. Tries to intervene and negate any subtle attacks by brawlers that make other people feel worthless. Has an artistic righteousness mindset.

<u>Susanna</u>

Is an OB-GYN doctor. Has two daughters and lives with her husband, Joakim, a wealthy society man. Is not resentful nor unhappy. Was born in Haifa. Is 34-years-old with a high, but not annoying, voice. Is considered to have a stunningly beautiful appearance. Has a Jewish clan mindset.

<u>David</u>

Is a judge. Likes beer and showbread. Plays several musical instruments, not the least of which is the harp. Does not require solemn oaths in the proceedings over which he presides. Is a mess of inconsistencies. Believes in the living, gracious God but resents fearing God. Confesses publicly. Hears stray voices. Repays good for evil, sometimes. Has a state conversioning mindset.

<u>Jesus</u>

Is a minister. Feels sorrow. Is not resentful. Imagines alternative ways of living. Takes extraordinary steps to be free from impingement. Values sanity. Overturns moneychangers' tables. Defeats death. Is a misopsémist. Sees capital's dangers. Has a conversioning mindset.

Jehoshaphat,
> Resents Joebh's sociopathic workplace criticism. Hears multiple voice streams. Has narrow eyes. Is prone to being a prosperity gospel cultist. Dreams of mass murder.

Onias,
> Resents Joebh at times, but is mentally-healthy enough to deflect/refute him. Is married to an adulteress. Believes that in the way of righteousness

is life. Is a former high priest in Jerusalem. Has
natural self-control that helps him to walk the talk.
Al Wayne,
Has difficulty understanding people with alternative
viewpoints. Resents personal scrutiny.
Mary, the sister-in-law,
Prefers to listen to teachings and to stories rather
than to help with the dishes. Is plain, naive, and
humble. Has some bad experiences, but is not
resentful.
Larry,
Is uncertain about whom his neighbors are. Is a
talkative and pragmatic lawyer. Resents invasive
dreams.
Joakim,
Accommodates court proceedings. Is on the
business council.
Judge 1,
Hears stray voices.
Judge 2,
Lusts for many women, but feels often cuckolded.
Steven,
Is a verbose, pragmatic lawyer who resents
abortionists and successful felos-de-se.
Kelli,
Has hair like a flock of goats and lips like a strand
of scarlet. Is tanned and has a waist like a heap of
wheat, tied in a string.
Mike,
Stunts potential by rejecting evil. Has eyes like
doves, black, wavy hair, and a body like carved
ivory. Resents jubilant people.

Counselor X,
    Admits mental illness is mainly caused by other
    people who are bullies.
Saul,
    Likes strife. Has a dad, Kish. Is handsome. Is awed
    by, but also resents, the unfairness of David.
Mary, the mom,
    Is a plot device.
Simeon,
    Is unhappy, blindly pious, and mentally ill. Wants a
    better future for Jews.
John the Baptist,
    Has reddish skin. Is sincere, elemental, and austere
    to a fault.
Some people,
    Have malleable minds.
Temple sellers,
    Resent the anger of Jesus.
Prosecutor,
    Resents his low pay for thankless work.
Peter,
    Resents the conflict avoidance attribute of himself.
    Is subservient. Has a brother, Andrew. Is from
    Bethsaida. Has ADHD.
Elijah,
    Defines justice as truthfulness about humans
    (historically) in relation to time, to other animals,
    and to aliens. Fasts and prays for an answer when
    he resents people who doubt his integrity. Is sad
    sometimes and is ready for his body to return to the
    earth.

June Lynnae,

Has interest in the inert earth and in economic benefits. Resents Judge 1 and Judge 2. Asks people, not the LORD, for advice. Likes Elijah.

Granddaughters,

Live with Susanna and Joakim.

Woman,

Resents Haggai's careless comment.

Students,

Taunt from fear.

Stephie,

Gets frazzled, but tries to stay calm.

Teacher 2,

Resents technological disturbances.

Teacher 3,

Resents working 60 hours a week.

Martha,

Demands Joebh's constant resourcefulness.

Jasmine,

Carries a melodic air horn distress device. Has black hair and dimples.

Adult sons and daughters,

Suffer from affluenza.

Traveler,

Parties with fervor.

Servants,

Help at Joebh's Jerusalem tenement.

Smith,

Resents Pierce Brosnan.

Wife,

Resents nature, and wants revenge, for the tragedies.

Mattathias,
> Is a reluctant leader who resents racism against his
> tribe. Loves pizza.

Antiochus Epiphanes,
> Resents Mattathias' "classy" classism
> noncompliance.

Army,
> Obeys Antiochus Epiphanes, with few gutsy
> exceptions.

Sons and kinsmen,
> Are faithful to Mattathias and to the tribe's
> traditions.

Index

Bel   https://s.surveyplanet.com/hesw95s9

1.

2.

3.

4.

5.   A man's current price & present value (PV) is calculated based on the expected future ascension of his penis and cash-flow acclivities.

	Strongly Disagree				Strongly Agree
	1	2	3	4	5
Agree or Disagree?					

6.

7.

8.

9.

10.   Your sexual intercourse (number of coital events, with other people, during lifetime):

        0 - 49?___   50 - 749?___

        750 - 1,999?___   2,000 - 14,999?___

        15,000 - 29,999?___   30,000 or more?___

11.

1.

2.

3.

4.   Misery is caused by the horror of genuflecting obedience. Men should serve, but never obey, because, as in economics, a free exchange creates a "wealthy" marriage.

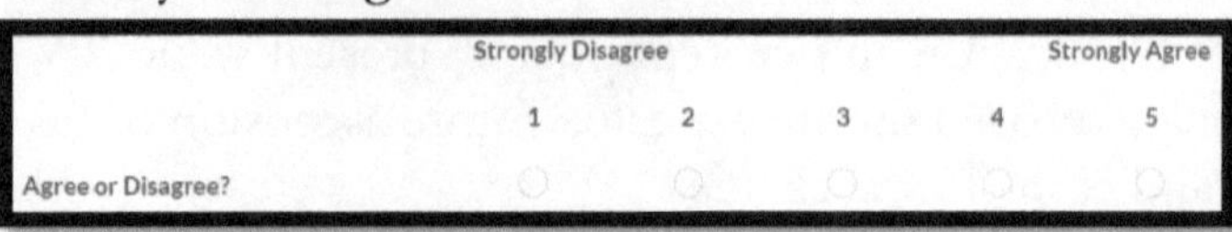

5.

6.

7.

8.

9.   Your sexual intercourse (number of coital events, with another person, in last six months):

0 - 9?___   10 - 49?___

50 - 149?___   150 or more?___

10.

11.

confused   https://s.surveyplanet.com/kts70x93

    1.

    2.

    3.   Passing the torch of painful living occurs by getting married & having children, which relieves your pain & passes it into your progeny.

<table>
<tr><td></td><td>Strongly Disagree</td><td></td><td></td><td></td><td>Strongly Agree</td></tr>
<tr><td></td><td>1</td><td>2</td><td>3</td><td>4</td><td>5</td></tr>
<tr><td>Agree or Disagree?</td><td></td><td></td><td></td><td></td><td></td></tr>
</table>

    4.

    5.

    6.

    7.

    8.   Your sex (now):
Female?______
Male?__________   Or?___________

    9.

    10.

    11.

eliminated   https://s.surveyplanet.com/i357qqxg
1.

2.   Wanting to have children & believing in
having children is to believe in Darwin's concept of "the
survival of the fittest." ("How are you?" is an evolutionary
shortcut question.) Not having children (or maybe only
one) is to believe in the God who wishes for us to believe
whole-heartedly in Him & to love one another. Not
wanting or having children might make the human race
weaker, maybe even leave more of a chance of extinction
(maybe), but it allows the chance for peace & love & reason
to flourish. To keep producing children might allow the
human race a greater chance of continuing, but it will be
the strong only who survive & the weak will be left to die
from disease, war, all types of violence, water pollution
(remember "water" is the future--"clean water," that is, for
the rich, the survivors)--hey, Why Live? And the Meaning
of Life is What?

3.
4.
5.
6.
7.   Your sex (at birth):
          Male?___________
          Female?________   Or?______________
8.
9.
10.
11.

establish   https://s.surveyplanet.com/y9xjo06j

1.   ¿Cuanto cuesta? should be the standard
pick-up line, whether it's for a date or for a
prostitute/gigolo. If the sexes are equal, anything else is a
complicit complot.

2.

3.

4.

5.

6.   Questionnaires prior to sexual relationships
would be the peaceful way, orderly, intelligent, assessing the
cost, hassle, etc. beforehand quantifiably.

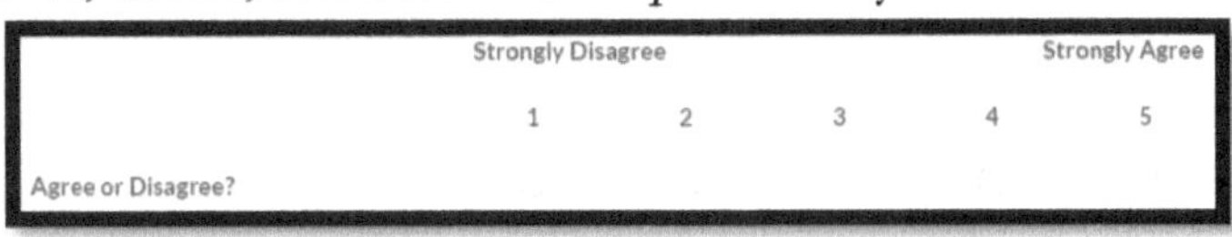

7.

8.

9.

10.

11.   Your age (now, in years):
        17 or less?__ 18 - 33?__ 34 - 49?__
        50 - 65?__ 66 or more?__

flow   https://s.surveyplanet.com/9qmlprm6

1.

2.

3.

4.

5.   Laconic women (& corporations) don't welcome a man until he accepts her (its) world, culture, premise & infects him with her (its) brand of localism.

6.

7.

8.

9.

10.   Your sexual intercourse (number of coital events, with other people, during lifetime):

0 - 49?___   50 - 749?___

750 - 1,999?___   2,000 - 14,999?___

15,000 - 29,999?___   30,000 or more?___

11.

generously		https://s.surveyplanet.com/x9hzd32o

1.

2.

3.

4.		Split-second nonverbal synchronicity in petting--the pace, the stages--is what a woman wants from a man, so she can enjoy the feelings while imagining how she can influence his life shortly.

	Strongly Disagree				Strongly Agree
	1	2	3	4	5
Agree or Disagree?					

5.

6.

7.

8.

9.		Your sexual intercourse (number of coital events, with another person, in last six months):

0 - 9?___   10 - 49?___

50 - 149?___   150 or more?___

10.

11.

Gethsemane   https://s.surveyplanet.com/iu1fct7t

1.

2.

3.   Uniting the biblical idea (Dispute), "You cannot serve God &" wealth (mammon), by morphing "wealth" & "mammon" into "women," gives "You cannot serve God & women," which is true, albeit a little Utopian.

Value

4.

5.

6.

7.

8.   Your sex (now):
Female?______
Male?_________   Or?___________

9.

10.

11.

greedy

https://s.surveyplanet.com/2213h31i

1.

2.   Desiring eyes interested in specific body parts (Leubh, English, libido, Latin desire) are the opposite of looking into another person's internal state of being (Leubh, English, galaubjan, German, belief, trust, esteem)-- listless? lost? filled with peace or filled with derision?

	Strongly Disagree				Strongly Agree
	1	2	3	4	5
Agree or Disagree?					

3.

4.

5.

6.

7.   Your sex (at birth):
Female?______
Male?________   Or?__________

8.

9.

10.

11.

         https://s.surveyplanet.com/mkgyo1vp

1.   Girls who are ugly (physically) make better wives--as Jimmy Soul's song "If You Wanna Be Happy" recommends: An ugly girl who marries a man (for the rest of his life) will make him the most glad & the least grudged.

2.

3.

4.

5.

6.   A law for land purchases is similar to a law for marriage. A woman is like land. It's gaia. It's the mother earth. Men like laws. It doesn't much matter to the earth. It does what it does no matter what laws there are.

7.

8.

9.

10.

11.   Your age (now, in years):
17 or less?___   18 - 33?___   34 - 49?___
50 - 65?___   66 or more?___

honeybuns   https://s.surveyplanet.com/xkfgj0c2
        1.
        2.
        3.
        4.
        5.   By confessing (not hiding) & living such
that others won't want to kill us, we can evolve into the
truth & ban the boogeyman.

Living unhid is desirable but unprofitable (for yourself).

Living unhid is a horrible idea that takes all the fun out of life.

Living unhid is desirable & a great way to make a lot of money (for yourself).

Other

        6.
        7.
        8.
        9.
        10.   Your sexual intercourse (number of coital
events, with other people, during lifetime):
                0 - 49?___   50 - 749?___
                750 - 1,999?___   2,000 - 14,999?___
                15,000 - 29,999?___ 30,000 or more?___
        11.

horses   https://s.surveyplanet.com/9k7gr88g
1.
2.
3.
4.   Ejaculation by masturbation means less lust & fewer shared sexual experiences, while less masturbation means more lust & a greater allotment of experience.

5.
6.
7.
8.
9.   Your sexual intercourse (number of coital events, with another person, in last six months):
0 - 9?__   10 - 49?__
50 - 149?__   150 or more?__
10.
11.

idols   https://s.surveyplanet.com/9m3mxoaq

    1.

    2.

    3.   When women share brains by talking & agreeing & trying to come to a final decision together, women are more successful & groupthinking wins.

Agree or Disagree?	Strongly Disagree				Strongly Agree
	1	2	3	4	5

    4.

    5.

    6.

    7.

    8.   Your sex (now):
Female?______
Male?__________   Or?___________

    9.

    10.

    11.

important	https://s.surveyplanet.com/gl5b2mk3

1.

2.	Surreptitious women enjoy kiss (sex) & tell sharing (including intimate details) with their best friends, sisters, & moms to achieve momentary stardom.

3.
4.
5.
6.
7.	Your sex (at birth):
	Female?______
	Male?_________		Or?___________
8.
9.
10.
11.

inspiration   https://s.surveyplanet.com/3776woco

1.   Out of many possibilities, if righteousness is the honest seeking of the perfect ideal (while confessing imperfection), what would be your ideal form of sexual perfection & optimization?

2.
3.
4.
5.
6.   Women mostly consider Jesus Christ as a competitor in bed (sexual activities) & prefer he's never around as a witness.

Value

7.
8.
9.
10.
11.   Your age (now, in years):
17 or less?__ 18 - 33?__ 34 - 49?__
50 - 65?__ 66 or more?__

instruments   https://s.surveyplanet.com/zel0sdh8
1.
2.
3.
4.
5.   Christian (or spiritual) women believe if they obey their feelings, they are obeying the LORD, the truth, & the universe (even if they don't understand a single Sunday morning concept of faith). For men, the truth is in their thoughts. Remembering this distinction helps prevent chafing.

6.
7.
8.
9.
10.   Your sexual intercourse (number of coital events, with other people, during lifetime):
0 - 49?___   50 - 749?___
750 - 1,999?___   2,000 - 14,999?___
15,000 - 29,999?___   30,000 or more?___
11.

insult   https://s.surveyplanet.com/dcxpk07h

1.
2.
3.
4.   If a person talks dirty in bed but doesn't talk dirty in church, this person has one faith, all of whose actions are easily integrated.

A person who talks dirty in bed , but does not talk dirty in church, is a person with integrity.

A person who talks dirty in bed, but does not talk dirty in church , is NOT a person with integrity.

A person's faith has no correlation to the actions in one's life, so trying to reconcile faith & integrity is absurd.

Other

5.
6.
7.
8.
9.   Your sexual intercourse (number of coital events, with another person, in last six months):
        0 - 9?___   10 - 49?___
        50 - 149?___   150 or more?___
10.
11.

intent   https://s.surveyplanet.com/a3fnlhw2

    1.

    2.

    3.   Do earth's women normally choose moneymakers, & love liars, but steer clear of eccentric outliers, who for them there is "no deal"?

    4.

    5.

    6.

    7.

    8.   Your sex (now):
Male?__________
Female?______   Or?____________

    9.

    10.

    11.

ivory   https://s.surveyplanet.com/314w22om
    1.
    2.   How many verses in the contemporary versions of the Judeo-Christian Bible (66 or 80 books) state that a man who protects the members of his household is fulfilling an obligation that is holy?

Value

    3.
    4.
    5.
    6.
    7.   Your sex (at birth):
              Male?_________
              Female?______   Or?___________
    8.
    9.
    10.
    11.

Jesus   https://s.surveyplanet.com/rb70dbmu

1.   For women, wanting protection is only an illusion to appeal to men's egos. In reality, women feel they can accomplish more in life when they have a man to boss around fussily.

	Strongly Disagree				Strongly Agree
	1	2	3	4	5
Agree or Disagree?	○	○	○	○	○

2.

3.

4.

5.

6.   Incentives for hard, good work make for strong civilizations, but greater freedom for women means the rewards of free women are given randomly & not on the basis of hard, honest work, & this randomness leads to falls in civilizations because of weak infrastructure.

- [ ] Incentives (& rewards) for hard, honest work build strong civilizations.
- [ ] Greater freedom for women means women's incentives & rewards (for men) are given for other reasons besides hard, honest work.
- [ ] Weak infrastructure signals the gradual demise of civilizations.
- [ ] Other

7.

8.

9.

10.

11.   Your age (now, in years):
17 or less?__ 18 - 33?__ 34 - 49?__
50 - 65?__ 66 or more?__

Joebh   https://s.surveyplanet.com/e5dyos5d

1.

2.

3.

4.

5.	Hookers use line of sight, hearing (voices), & smell (perfume) trapping tactics, which are the same methods of seducing & luring used by all women ex hypothesi.

	Strongly Disagree				Strongly Agree
	1	2	3	4	5
Agree or Disagree?					

6.

7.

8.

9.

10.	Your sexual intercourse (number of coital events, with other people, during lifetime):

0 - 49?___   50 - 749?___

750 - 1,999?___   2,000 - 14,999?___

15,000 - 29,999?___   30,000 or more?___

11.

land https://s.surveyplanet.com/nbnl37kc

1.

2.

3.

4. Doctrines of virtuous, unmarried women's behavior don't exist because unmarried women largely rely on Cosmopolitan magazine which teaches how to be "worldly" (Kosmos = world, Greek) disciples.

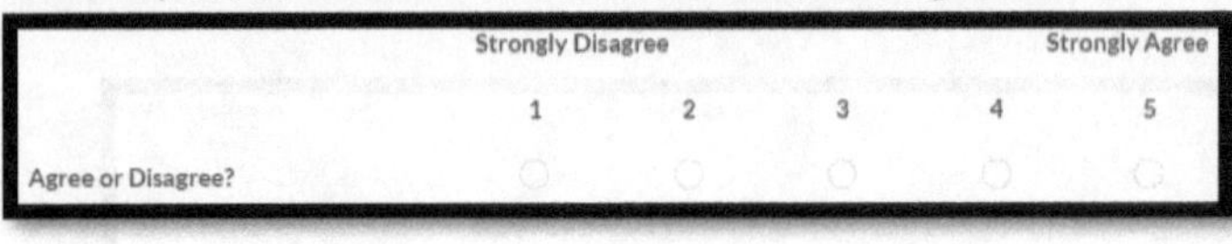

5.

6.

7.

8.

9. Your sexual intercourse (number of coital events, with another person, in last six months):
0 - 9?__ 10 - 49?__
50 - 149?__ 150 or more?__

10.

11.

lawyer   https://s.surveyplanet.com/fqldebay
    1.
    2.
    3.   When our sexual activity, flaws, & physiques remain hidden behind clothes & private doors, the gain from this intentional obscurity is mostly whose?

People with a lot of sexual activity.

People with physical disabilities.

People whose physiques (unclothed) differ from their preferred personas.

Other

    4.
    5.
    6.
    7.
    8.   Your sex (now):
            Female?______
            Male?__________   Or?____________
    9.
    10.
    11.

lazy   https://s.surveyplanet.com/ukh9a8he
  1.
  2. They can be women, or they can be equal, but presuming they can be both is too functionally absurd & trite.

Agree or Disagree?	Strongly Disagree				Strongly Agree
	1	2	3	4	5
	○	○	○	○	○

  3.
  4.
  5.
  6.
  7. Your sex (at birth):
Male?__________
Female?______   Or?___________
  8.
  9.
  10.
  11.

lend   https://s.surveyplanet.com/2f3fky4o

1.   Hardly ever does an intimate relationship begin with seriousness: (1) humor makes women feel good "in the present moment," & (2) there is an evolutionary skill evident when a man can be hammy.

<table>
<tr><td></td><td>Strongly Disagree</td><td></td><td></td><td></td><td>Strongly Agree</td></tr>
<tr><td></td><td>1</td><td>2</td><td>3</td><td>4</td><td>5</td></tr>
<tr><td>Agree or Disagree?</td><td></td><td></td><td></td><td></td><td></td></tr>
</table>

2.

3.

4.

5.

6.   Happiness for women is second by second. If she's having fun, she's happy. If the next second she's not having fun, then she's unhappy. For men, happiness is more evened out across time, more mindful & less pulled moment by moment by the heartstrings.

<table>
<tr><td></td><td>Strongly Disagree</td><td></td><td></td><td></td><td>Strongly Agree</td></tr>
<tr><td></td><td>1</td><td>2</td><td>3</td><td>4</td><td>5</td></tr>
<tr><td>Agree or Disagree?</td><td></td><td></td><td></td><td></td><td></td></tr>
</table>

7.

8.

9.

10.

11.   Your age (now, in years):
17 or less?__   18 - 33?__   34 - 49?__
50 - 65?__   66 or more?__

loosen   https://s.surveyplanet.com/7c64r37d

1.

2.

3.

4.

5.   Are you aware of the perverse incentives that commonly cause people to misbehave & lie? Please aver.

6.

7.

8.

9.

10.   Your sexual intercourse (number of coital events, with other people, during lifetime):

0 - 49?__   50 - 749?__
750 - 1,999?__   2,000 - 14,999?__
15,000 - 29,999?__ 30,000 or more?__

11.

1.

2.

3.

4.   Knowing what is considered sexually immoral makes everything ELSE kosher.

5.

6.

7.

8.

9.   Your sexual intercourse (number of coital events, with another person, in last six months):

0 - 9?__   10 - 49?__

50 - 149?__   150 or more?__

10.

11.

lovingkindness   https://s.surveyplanet.com/acipbv5u

1.

2.

3.   Creepy women do not like excessively truthful men, because women are devious creatures & birds of a feather flock together closely.

<table>
<tr><td>Agree or Disagree?</td><td>Strongly Disagree</td><td></td><td></td><td></td><td>Strongly Agree</td></tr>
<tr><td></td><td>1</td><td>2</td><td>3</td><td>4</td><td>5</td></tr>
</table>

4.

5.

6.

7.

8.   Your sex (now):
Male?__________
Female?______   Or?____________

9.

10.

11.

Mary   https://s.surveyplanet.com/w5yhh0h9

    1.

    2.   Predominant predispositions related to how & when children pick up sexual tidbits could be managed more successfully to avoid baggage & the beginning of perversity.

Agree or Disagree?	Strongly Disagree				Strongly Agree
	1	2	3	4	5

    3.

    4.

    5.

    6.

    7.   Your sex (at birth):
Male?__________
Female?______   Or?____________

    8.

    9.

    10.

    11.

mercy   https://s.surveyplanet.com/k6vwaegm

1.   If men's & women's bodies were created to fit together & give pleasure, wouldn't nature have planned men's & women's spirits to fit together & give pleasure also? Why are we so far off from nature's intention, often being forced to bear the brunt of the ill will this misalignment inveighs?

2.

3.

4.

5.

6.   Free dates should be doled out (by men) to women whose underlying beliefs, common attitudes, & life goals are known beforehand to be in sync, rather than to women with pretty boobs, just in case there's a slight chance the latter have these in-sync fundamentals.

	Strongly Disagree				Strongly Agree
	1	2	3	4	5
Agree or Disagree?	○	○	○	○	○

7.

8.

9.

10.

11.   Your age (now, in years):
17 or less?__ 18 - 33?__ 34 - 49?__
50 - 65?__ 66 or more?__

messenger   https://s.surveyplanet.com/aoj4u664
1.
2.
3.
4.
5.   Some conservative men prefer "purchasing" women (long-term prostitution), other men prefer "rent-to-own" agreements (living together unmarried), while some liberal men think "renting" a woman (short-term prostitution) makes the most sense.

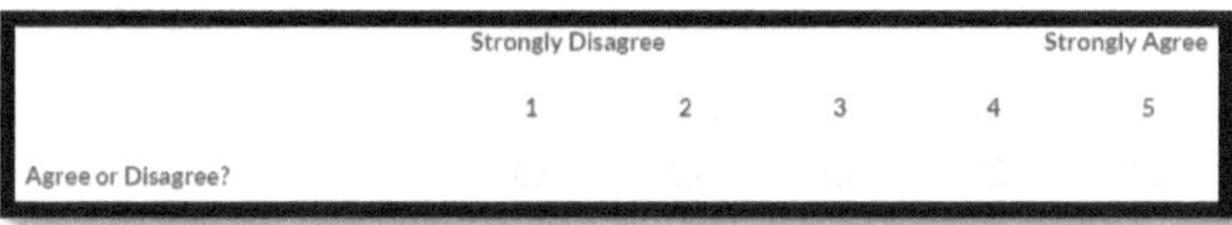

6.
7.
8.
9.
10.   Your sexual intercourse (number of coital events, with other people, during lifetime):
0 - 49?__   50 - 749?__
750 - 1,999?__   2,000 - 14,999?__
15,000 - 29,999?__   30,000 or more?__
11.

moneychangers https://s.surveyplanet.com/hl0y21eq

1.
2.
3.
4. Capricious lying ordinarily will give people lives filled with more money & less cheeriness.

- [ ] Capricious lying often is a way to make more money.
- [ ] Capricious lying often makes a person less cheery.
- [ ] Other

5.
6.
7.
8.
9. Your sexual intercourse (number of coital events, with another person, in last six months):

    0 - 9?__ 10 - 49?__
    50 - 149?__ 150 or more?__

10.
11.

nourishment   https://s.surveyplanet.com/sb5hmgsw

1.

2.

3.   Much of what women give to an amatory relationship is enticement & incentive. Is what women give (& men receive) equal in value to what men give (& women receive) on the amatory scoreboard marquee?

What women give is less in value than what men give.

What men give is less in value than what women give.

What women give is approximately equal in value to what men give.

Other

4.

5.

6.

7.

8.   Your sex (now):
Male?__________
Female?______   Or?___________

9.

10.

11.

offended   https://s.surveyplanet.com/l51odc9a
      1.
      2.   By learning to look at PYTs at the right
time, with the right stare, for the right amount of time, with
the right feeling, with the right sensitivity to nearby women,
by enjoying without having or wanting, there would be less
assault & battery.

      3.
      4.
      5.
      6.
      7.   Your sex (at birth):
                  Male?__________
                  Female?______   Or?____________
      8.
      9.
      10.
      11.

perpetually   https://s.surveyplanet.com/vu33c7y3
    1.   To walk up to a woman & say, "May I kiss you?," would likely cause a reaction in her tantamount to...

Extreme happiness?

Extreme unhappiness?

Extreme excitement?

Extreme revulsion?

All 4 (above) feelings at the same time?

Other

    2.
    3.
    4.
    5.
    6.   Love & hate are nonsense, nondescript words. Calling women "users" & men "sexers" would clear things up & help us communicate sincerely, or reliably, leastways.

	Strongly Disagree				Strongly Agree
	1	2	3	4	5
Agree or Disagree?					

    7.
    8.
    9.
    10.
    11.   Your age (now, in years):
17 or less?___ 18 - 33?___ 34 - 49?___
50 - 65?___ 66 or more?___

plowshares   https://s.surveyplanet.com/55w7hcyn

1.

2.

3.

4.

5.   Peaceful existence for a man is represented by the ancient yin-yang symbol, along with the way that women inflict drama into any given situation at her peril.

6.

7.

8.

9.

10.   Your sexual intercourse (number of coital events, with other people, during lifetime):

0 - 49?___   50 - 749?___

750 - 1,999?___   2,000 - 14,999?___

15,000 - 29,999?___ 30,000 or more?___

11.

reputation   https://s.surveyplanet.com/ooiqpdqb

1.

2.

3.

4.   Funny are liars, but truthers are somber & fusty.

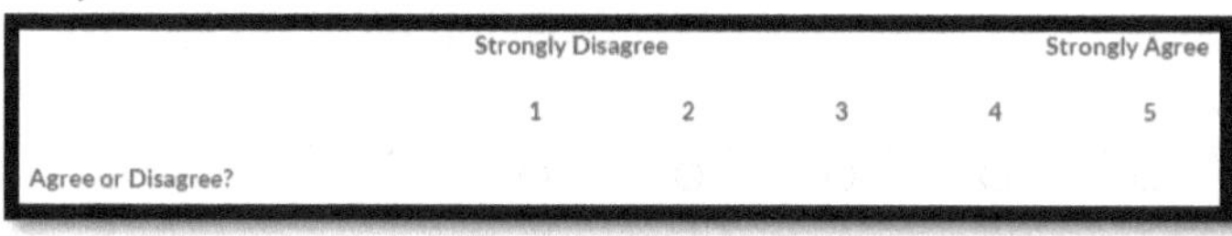

5.

6.

7.

8.

9.   Your sexual intercourse (number of coital events, with another person, in last six months):

0 - 9?___   10 - 49?___

50 - 149?___   150 or more?___

10.

11.

righteousness   https://s.surveyplanet.com/xah5opyc

     1.

     2.

     3.   Nowadays women marry for pleasure & other useful commodities, divorces are allowed at whim, child support payments are established, vague sexual harassment laws are passed, & men's interests are left for naught.

	Strongly Disagree				Strongly Agree
	1	2	3	4	5
Agree or Disagree?	○	○	○	○	○

     4.

     5.

     6.

     7.

     8.   Your sex (now):
Female?______
Male?________   Or?__________

     9.

     10.

     11.

robbed   https://s.surveyplanet.com/k1hgxrpb

1.

2.   The four top women's behaviors that cause men to throw temper tantrums:

3.

4.

5.

6.

7.   Your sex (at birth):
          Male?__________
          Female?______   Or?____________

8.

9.

10.

11.

strife   https://s.surveyplanet.com/vg3pl57f

1.   Animal magnetism brings men's & women's bodies together. If not for disagreements (repulsive energy) in men's & women's spirits, we would collapse inwardly & implode into a central heap of inactivity. Some balance on earth is kept by the disagreements that keep us apart.

	Strongly Disagree				Strongly Agree
	1	2	3	4	5
Agree or Disagree?	○	○	○	○	○

2.

3.

4.

5.

6.   Give an explanation of good & faultless routines that are acceptable both to a man & to a woman & leave no trace of any griping or grimacing.

7.

8.

9.

10.

11.   Your age (now, in years):
17 or less?___ 18 - 33?___ 34 - 49?___
50 - 65?___ 66 or more?___

suspicious   https://s.surveyplanet.com/b4a8r9po

    1.

    2.

    3.

    4.

    5.   Honesty (for a woman) is not breached unless you ask: "Did you touch, kiss, blow, or fuck someone today?" To avoid hell (a hellish existence), one's happy condition must be confronted frequently (daily?), because the origin of the Anglo-Saxon word "hell" means "to cover, to conceal, to hide."

Daily asking (a wife or girlfriend) if they were intimate with someone else is awkward, but necessary (to maintain a relationship).

Daily asking (a wife or girlfriend) if they were intimate with someone else is NOT necessary (to maintain a relationship).

Other

    6.

    7.

    8.

    9.

    10.   Your sexual intercourse (number of coital events, with other people, during lifetime):

0 - 49?__   50 - 749?__

750 - 1,999?__   2,000 - 14,999?__

15,000 - 29,999?__   30,000 or more?__

    11.

thighs   https://s.surveyplanet.com/fhpjtayi
1.
2.
3.
4.   Nasty actions such as harassment & rape should sensibly be expected in a society where hate & love is a fun game most nauseous.

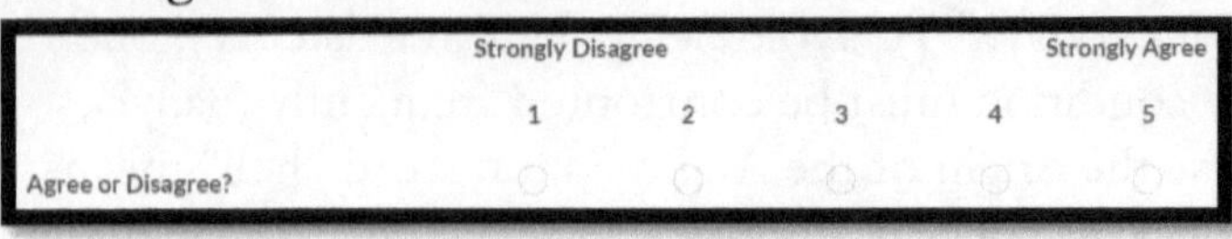

5.
6.
7.
8.
9.   Your sexual intercourse (number of coital events, with another person, in last six months):
0 - 9?___   10 - 49?___
50 - 149?___   150 or more?___
10.
11.

touches   https://s.surveyplanet.com/vjy1nmg9

     1.

     2.

     3.   Regular girls choose bad boys, therefore men choose not to be righteous.

	Strongly Disagree				Strongly Agree
	1	2	3	4	5
Agree or Disagree?					

     4.

     5.

     6.

     7.

     8.   Your sex (now):
Male?__________
Female?______   Or?___________

     9.

     10.

     11.

traveler   https://s.surveyplanet.com/f19myf3a
      1.
      2.   Does paying a woman to practice all of the various sex steps help a man to know what he's getting into, so, later, he doesn't unpredictably jump ship & disappear?

Value

      3.
      4.
      5.
      6.
      7.   Your sex (at birth):
              Female?______
              Male?__________   Or?____________
      8.
      9.
      10.
      11.

twists   https://s.surveyplanet.com/053v15hh

1.   Perfect phoniness cordons one's sex life from one's daylife to avoid awkward, knavish confrontations on the work premises.

2.

3.

4.

5.

6.   Yin-yang relationships are dramatic wars. When wives & girlfriends know how much men truly "love" them, women have too much leverage, which is why men have to resist sex sometimes, to avoid getting manipulated like blundering yo-yos.

7.

8.

9.

10.

11.   Your age (now, in years):
17 or less?___   18 - 33?___   34 - 49?___
50 - 65?___   66 or more?___

1.

2.

3.

4.

5.   By accepting an unsolicited blowjob, a man accepts a bribe. A righteous man should not accept bribes. Righteousness & sexuality are generally opposites that make their reconciliation logistically baffling.

	Strongly Disagree				Strongly Agree
	1	2	3	4	5
Agree or Disagree?	○	○	○	○	○

6.

7.

8.

9.

10.   Your sexual intercourse (number of coital events, with other people, during lifetime):

       0 - 49?___   50 - 749?___

       750 - 1,999?___   2,000 - 14,999?___

       15,000 - 29,999?___   30,000 or more?___

11.

vegetables   https://s.surveyplanet.com/a2twzpsb

1.

2.

3.

4.   By getting married, is lust for one's spouse increased or decreased, & is lust for others (not one's spouse) lowered or boosted?

> After marriage, lust increased for one's spouse but lowered towards others.
>
> After marriage, lust decreased for one's spouse & also lowered towards others.
>
> After marriage, lust increased for one's spouse & also boosted towards others.
>
> After marriage, lust decreased for one's spouse but boosted towards others.
>
> Other

5.

6.

7.

8.

9.   Your sexual intercourse (number of coital events, with another person, in last six months):

0 - 9?___   10 - 49?___

50 - 149?___   150 or more?___

10.

11.

1.

2.

3.   Ordinarily, winning a woman through seriousness is fruitless. If a woman is attracted to a man, she giggles & doesn't think clearly--this should be obvious.

	Strongly Disagree				Strongly Agree
	1	2	3	4	5
Agree or Disagree?	○	○	○	○	○

4.

5.

6.

7.

8.   Your sex (now):
Male?__________
Female?______   Or?___________

9.

10.

11.

Appendix B: Noah's Skills

1st	Assail a whopper
2nd	Drive a flying car
3rd	Cook a frozen glop to perfection
4th	Discuss confirmation bias with intelligence
5th	Discuss optimism bias with intelligence
6th	Craft a neon signboard
7th	Calculate option prices using Black-Scholes
8th	Blend ghrelin hormones for fillip therapy
9th	Transform stress situations into benign ones
10th	Self-propel a moon trip excursion
11th	Dress a turkey
12th	Dress smashingly for success
13th	Swim a combat side stroke
14th	Pen a comedy
15th	Finance a comedy performance
16th	Diagram the pine-cone reproduction cycle
17th	Catch a sea snake
18th	Ride a blue shark
19th	Deliver historical TV tidbits like, "God has a plan for you, Gaius. He has a plan for everything and everyone" (Number Six).
20th	Ameliorate dysregulation disorder
21st	Apply a tourniquet
22nd	Beat a polygraph
23rd	Operate an open miter
24th	Purify potable water from human excretions
25th	Shoe a horse
26th	Assimilate new information effortlessly
27th	Describe Caesar's Middlesex invasion until the Roman founding of London
28th	Build a kerkis (church) triangular odeon

29th	Dance a tango
30th	Learn from patients' experiences
31st	Write a logillogram
32nd	Compose a dirge
33rd	Helm a junk
34th	Demonstrate the delusion of deathlessness
35th	Monitor performance and correct as needed
36th	Survive a biological warfare attack
37th	Draw a troodon
38th	Grow butterworts
39th	Carbon date a fossil
40th	Tie a bowknot
41st	Manufacture a balloon bicycle
42nd	Debunk a gripe
43rd	Detail how domestic abuse is caused by women in over 95% of cases, even though women accept around 0% of the blame
44th	Grill a savory barbecued monkfish
45th	Gather idiographic data into discernible frameworks like Mendeleev's periodic table
46th	Depict a biophoton's role in consciousness
47th	Write for the needs of a particular audience
48th	Identify active, or passive, illicit sexual abuse
49th	Expound that if Harlow's pit of despair is unethical, so is it unethical to tell lonely and hopeless humans that Life Is Good
50th	Scale a redwood (legally)
51st	Explain the meter-size barrier snag
52nd	Plunder a miscreant normally
53rd	Construct an impenetrable egoistic facade
54th	Break the sound barrier with a whip
55th	Construct a wind-turbine generator
56th	Convey information effectively verbally
57th	Leap a loveseat in a single bound

58th	Fake concern
59th	Recite Ed Bellamy's chapter nine by heart
60th	Tie a killer Prusik knot
61st	Clean dishes without leaving water spots
62nd	Moderate the sexual lurch to avoid nimiety
63rd	Sidestep sex miscommunications with verity
64th	Transmit sexual steps vocally beforehand
65th	Neglect mindless heterogeneity in sex acts
66th	Penetrate and ejaculate without any frills
67th	Sing La Donna è Mobile
68th	Fashion a cup out of aluminum
69th	Use SPSS for significance analysis
70th	Iron a silk necktie
71st	Track adenosine and dopamine levels for 6σ
72nd	Perceive others' reasons for their reactions
73rd	Taper passive-aggressive inclinations
74th	Climb a wall like a gecko with grab gloves
75th	Treat rational, upstairs brain issues
76th	Sleep like a log
77th	Smell a tamandua a mile away
78th	Run a 10K in under 50 minutes
79th	Translate functional MRIs
80th	Discern threats in dreams
81st	Examine alternative solutions
82nd	Outwit impetuosity with silence healing
83rd	Defang virtual influencer malady (VIM)
84th	Plan remote bio-monitoring for patients
85th	Eat a whole fifth of durian without puking
86th	Cultivate a garden
87th	Order dishes from a menu in Italian
88th	Read a balance sheet
89th	Play the ukulele
90th	Shear a sheep
91st	Spark a fire with sunlight

92nd	Determine and divide moral intelligence from emotional intelligence
93rd	Shoot a particle-beam rifle
94th	Make candles
95th	Expound the ring of Gyges
96th	Understand human uprisings
97th	Troubleshoot a smart toilet
98th	Build a wattle fence
99th	Entertain children
100th	Soothe technological stress
101st	Fabricate a pain-subsiding tincture
102nd	Rely on seven income streams for cash flow
103rd	Disentangle mindless frantic world interactions
104th	Render animal fat
105th	Dabble in ethology
106th	Replace a solar panel
107th	Operate a Dr. Car Robot
108th	Braid a rug
109th	Ski a black diamond hill
110th	Serve caviar on a blini
111th	Sharpen a chainsaw
112th	Mull reality
113th	Preserve brain expertise of Broca's area
114th	Recognize unspoken body language clues
115th	Build a stepping-stone path
116th	Err less than average
117th	Name the four main brain sutures
118th	Controvert the existence of kleptoparasitism
119th	Use rennet to make cream cheese
120th	Express complicated ideas in simple ways
121st	Encourage reasonable cultural objections
122nd	Dig clams

123rd	Describe how false pleasures are unsatisfying
124th	Detail the harms of impersonal philanthropy
125th	Make a medicinal infusion
126th	Grow fuel in a greenhouse
127th	Read complicated research results deftly
128th	Identify birds by their singing
129th	Be a team leader
130th	Increase self-control in patients by chemical means
131st	Trot a horse
132nd	Describe Swedenborg-Kant-Laplace star formation theories
133rd	Sew a tote bag
134th	Blanch vegetables
135th	Increase self-esteem in patients by truthful means
136th	Proceed assertively
137th	Camp
138th	Extract honey from a beehive
139th	Give false impressions with spin
140th	Publish in journals such as *Death Studies*
141st	Harvest rainwater
142nd	Employ the maieutic method
143rd	Repair concrete cracks
144th	Make beef jerky
145th	Dispense the 28 nano-steps for animal sex
146th	Send signals at a distance by controlling thoughts
147th	Explain the hypothetical imperatives
148th	Arrange misinformation without uneasiness
149th	Fix a broken windowpane
150th	Tie a clove hitch

151st	Measure scale of delusion
152nd	Build an outdoor shower
153rd	Nosh a protein-rich dry-roasted cricket
154th	Talk small
155th	Add value to any scene or situation
156th	Identify six different owl hoots
157th	Posit sociological causes of dipsomania
158th	Install a foundation French drain
159th	Reconnoiter a data bank
160th	Build a cordwood wall
161st	Show flexibility in grouping standard traits
162nd	Ponder moksha
163rd	Change a bicycle tire
164th	Scale tremendous heights fearlessly
165th	Monitor truthfulness of conversations in formal settings
166th	Navigate by celestial objects
167th	Exhibit ataraxia
168th	Analyze cost-benefit opportunities
169th	Suture a deep cut
170th	Produce fresh sausage
171st	Expose carefully-edited dishonesty theories
172nd	Allay awkward situations
173rd	Make shingle repairs on a roof
174th	Treat rashes with the right weeds
175th	Define "caring community" boundaries
176th	Calculate Lagrangian L_1, L_2, L_3, L_4, and L_5
177th	Offer inventive solutions for predicaments
178th	Grow upside-down vegetables in a bucket
179th	Refute Sittlichkeit
180th	Discuss Descartes brilliantly
181st	Identify root cause(s) of complex problems
182nd	Carve a turkey
183rd	Prescribe vasopressin remedies

184th	Trim a mustache
185th	Fashion a paper lantern
186th	Install a tile floor
187th	Explain how Fichte's ethics distinguishes between a sociopath and a beautiful soul
188th	Coordinate activities in relation to others'
189th	Construct a homemade water filter
190th	Escape a wild boar
191st	Construct a training rotocopter
192nd	Imagine dystopian settings as an antidote for ennui
193rd	Grow elephant-foot yams
194th	Make paper
195th	Play the Danish gambit
196th	Argue emphatically for Dignity in Dying
197th	Smoke meat on the stove
198th	Prescribe psilocybin for neurotics
199th	Support people susceptible to homelessness through pro bono advisory services
200th	Brew beer
201st	Kill a hen
202nd	Flip a complaint into a simple request
203rd	Hang a floating shelf
204th	Select proper mental teaching methods
205th	Walk with abandon
206th	Make bitters
207th	Expedite pattern recognition
208th	Communicate original position justice
209th	Expostulate childish adults
210th	Hang a tire swing
211th	Construct a poncho liner shelter
212th	Sift criticism
213th	Make a laundry/landscape graywater system
214th	Use rhetoric to manipulate others' behavior

215th   Fix a drywall hole
216th   Create clever solutions to unusual problems
217th   Debone a trout
218th   Bake bread in a flowerpot
219th   Facilitate discussion of whether Hume
             meant thought or feeling when examining
             his use of force and vivacity
220th   Point out antilogisms
221st   Adjust tone of voice applicably
222nd   Identify animal tracks
223rd   Revert time
224th   Outline supersymmetry
225th   Change an automobile tire
226th   Maintain focus when facing arduous tasks
227th   Sift Husserl
228th   Install a ceiling track marquee
229th   Build a tin can stove
230th   Clear a jungle path
231st   Launch a 5-person hydrogen balloon
232nd   Negotiate to bring others to a set opinion
233rd   Raise a log cabin
234th   Help protect the public against
             unreasonable use of dangerous inventions
             through intervention procedures
235th   Counsel life prolongation applicants
236th   Instruct others with tact and discretion
237th   Spatchcock a chicken
238th   Find the center of a circle
239th   Isolate hidden mental degenerative causes
240th   Install under-cabinet lighting
241st   Replace a car battery
242nd   Grasp veridical perceptions
243rd   Regulate time to fulfill one's affairs
244th   Fundraise for societal improvements

245th	Make cheddar cheese
246th	Arrange a funeral
247th	Recognize socialization contrivances
248th	Replace a defunct heat joth hopper chute
249th	Organize a clambake
250th	Identify twenty-five distinct ladybug species
251st	Grill frog legs
252nd	Give a full-body massage
253rd	Install a dimmer switch
254th	Assess personality and behavioral disorders
255th	Perform nimbly when clear rules are absent
256th	Make sauerkraut
257th	Inform patients of ways to defend against being exploited
258th	Debate the four idols of the tribe, den, market, and theatre
259th	Grow an espalier
260th	Move adeptly from ideas to treatments for patients
261st	Explain the wasp-fig symbiotic relationship
262nd	Ponder the best of all possible worlds 150,000 years in the future
263rd	Hang a hammock
264th	Urge reasoned conation
265th	Draw an Escher
266th	Retain composure in high-stress settings
267th	Fix a burst pipe
268th	Use principles and procedures for diagnosis
269th	Disarm logomachies
270th	Recaulk a bathtub
271st	Rewire an oscilloscope
272nd	Administer CPR
273rd	List the 180 known scales of talent
274th	Reupholster a seat

275th	Can gooseberry jam
276th	Treat perfluoroalkyl and polyfluoroalkyl substance in patients to reduce deaths by suicide
277th	Make a compost pile
278th	Adjust prosody
279th	Impress with fashionable designer clothes
280th	Exhibit niceties in decorum
281st	Can probiotic pickles
282nd	Transform patients with orectic problems
283rd	Concoct a gourmet baked potato
284th	Diagnose shallow and dishonest social anxiety disorder (SAD)
285th	Administer transcranial DC stimulation
286th	Fix tempeh
287th	Install ultraviolet water filtration
288th	Reach conclusions by dialectic
289th	Change a motorcycle tire
290th	Evaluate quality of patients' satisfaction
291st	Explain how conscientiousness is a deal-breaker in many venues
292nd	Mantel an overhang
293rd	Walk like an Egyptian
294th	Tap a maple tree
295th	Recommend entelechy thinking and doing
296th	Generate opposition to excessive disparity in human incomes
297th	Engage in Gedankenexperimente
298th	Fulfill obligations that can't be shelved
299th	Make biodiesel fuel
300th	Navigate Godthåb Fjord
301st	Adapt treatment to the individual needs of patients
302nd	Repair a centerset faucet

303rd	Ask the important, relevant questions
304th	Stitch leather lederhosen
305th	Weave a basket
306th	Explicate the Copenhagen interpretation
307th	Drink water from a plantain tree
308th	Compose articulate linguistic content
309th	Assist the government in fighting narcotics crimes through profile analysis
310th	Glue and clamp a bookshelf in a vise
311th	Incubate Greek yogurt
312th	Argue the meaning of respect for persons
313th	Iron
314th	Utilize magnets in fingertips for odd jobs
315th	Float for survival
316th	Re-cover a lampshade
317th	Make kombucha
318th	Repair a window screen
319th	Appear as an interactive hologram at work
320th	Identify basic geological structures
321st	Impute nonresponses to survey questions by replacing with the mean of the variable
322nd	Parse parsimony and the simplest route to achieve a goal
323rd	Keep an axe sharp
324th	Understand cultures and their origins
325th	Manage brain uploads
326th	Solve predicaments heuristically
327th	Permit other people's freedomness
328th	Trade a credit-default swap
329th	Create mental acts
330th	Filter swamp water
331st	Construct a terrarium
332nd	Dictate 190 words per minute
333rd	Interpret Fichte's doctrine of Oikeiosis

334th	Fix a sticking door
335th	Convert shit, waste, garbage, and pollution
336th	Think in Boolean algebra terms
337th	Honor delayed gratification
338th	Teach consciousness theories
339th	Field dress a deer
340th	Sing the body electric
341st	Portray negative facts positively
342nd	Prune a Dragon's blood tree
343rd	Use Buridan's ass as a treatment argument for neurotics
344th	Craft a turnbuckle rattler perimeter alarm
345th	Do executive coaching with regard to employee/employer alignment
346th	Grow a garden with straw bales
347th	Wield a hydraulic potato squasher
348th	Ascertain infection causes and influences
349th	Model algorithmic decision procedures
350th	Hang a ceiling fan
351st	Deliver information cogently
352nd	Build a flowerpot smoker
353rd	Spell out Peirce's, Dewey's, and James' tenets of pragmatism
354th	Maintain cutting-edge research awareness
355th	Verbalize various phenomena that are typically indescribable
356th	Formulate possible future avenues
357th	Assist in the riddance of family dysfunction
358th	Explore resentment and ressentiment
359th	Complete paperwork drudgery efficiently
360th	Navigate using plants and trees
361st	Clean up after making a mess
362nd	Build an outdoor fire pit
363rd	Perform perlocutionary acts

364th	Distinguish between building illth and engineering moral camaraderie
365th	Dissect paradiastoles
366th	Install a thermostatic valve
367th	Synchronize groups without deceit
368th	Use logic
369th	Receive standing ovations at intellectual freedom conferences
370th	Lead group pacification sessions
371st	Extrapolate the future from present trends
372nd	Temper derailed experiences by journaling
373rd	Master a panic episode
374th	Request assistance with legal codes amicably
375th	Assemble an Atmoph Window
376th	Shuck an oyster
377th	Behave like a friend
378th	Dance bamboo tinikling
379th	Guide community progeniture maintenance efforts
380th	Persist in facing troubling discoveries
381st	Determine and separate positive statement (facts) from positive (upbeat) statements
382nd	Stream video signals through a teleporter
383rd	Subdue customized artificially-intelligent target marketing stress
384th	Practice Einfühlung for patients
385th	Insulate an attic
386th	Avoid hypothermia
387th	Observe customs from various theologies
388th	Neutralize a knife attacker
389th	Dulcify marketing manipulation stress
390th	Assist conflict resolution
391st	Help patients reduce their carbon footprint
392nd	Identify the poop of predators

393rd	Elucidate the causal linkage of personal identity
394th	Slice a mean backhand
395th	Investigate quandarious work uncertainties
396th	Perform staff reviews with care
397th	Handle heredity discussions
398th	Compute percentage of bullshit
399th	Build an elevated swamp bed
400th	Replace a bathroom fan

100 deadly skills
Author: Clint Emerson
Publisher: New York : Touchstone, ©2016

Aging and the Germ Line: Where Mortality and Immortality Meet
Author: D. Leanne Jones
Publisher: *Stem cell rev.* Humana press inc. ©2007. doi: 10.1007/s12015-007-0009-3. (Accessed January 11, 2023 from https://www.researchgate.net/profile/Leanne-Jones-10/publication/5928145_Aging_and_the_Germ_Line_Where_Mortality _and_Immortality_Meet/links/02e7e5187f6bd2fa88000000/Aging-and-the-Germ-Line-Where-Mortality-and-Immortality-Meet.pdf)

Audacious & outrageous : space elevators
Author: Steve Price
Publisher: NASA.gov. ©2000. (Accessed November 4, 2022 from https://science.nasa.gov/science-news/science-at-nasa/2000/ast07sep_1)

Best plays of the seventies
Author: Brian Clark (Whose life is it anyway?)
Publisher: Garden City, N.Y. : Doubleday, ©1980

DNA is not destiny : the remarkable, completely misunderstood relationship between you and your genes
Author: Steven J. Heine
Publisher: New York : W. W. Norton, ©2017

Essential home skills handbook : everything you need to know as a new homeowner
Author: Chris Peterson
Publisher: Beverly, MA : Cool Springs Press, ©2022

Hegel's Antigone
Author: Patricia J. Mills
Publisher: *The owl of Minerva*, Volume 17(2), pp.131-152, ©1986

Just Another Holy Book
Author: M. S. Marty
Publisher: Get a JAHB, LLC, ©2018

Litigations and the obstetrician in clinical practice
Author: J. Adinma
Publisher: *Ann med health sci res.* Mar-Apr;6(2):74-9. ©2016. doi: 10.4103/2141-9248.181847. PMID: 27213088; PMCID: PMC4866370. (Accessed October 25, 2022 from https://
www.ncbi.nlm.nih.gov/pmc/articles/PMC4866370/)

Nuclear integrations : challenges for mitochondrial DNA markers
Authors: D. X. Zhang and G. M. Hewitt
Publisher: *Trends in ecology & evolution*, 11(6), 247-251, ©1996

One hundred years of laws in psychology
Author: Karl Halvor Teigen
Publisher: *The American journal of psychology*, 115 (1) DOI: 10.2307/1423676 ©2002. (Accessed September 16, 2013 from https://alexholcombe.wordpress.com/

2011/11/19/top-15-most-popular-laws-in-psychology-journal-abstracts/)

Oxford dictionary of philosophy
Author: Simon Blackburn
Publisher: Oxford University Press, ©2016

Public school expenditures : condition of education.
Author: U.S. Department of Education, Institute of Education Sciences
Publisher: National center for education statistics. ©2022. (Accessed October 27, 2022 from https://nces.ed.gov/programs/coe/indicator/cmb)

RL Stevenson's "strange case of Dr. Jekyll and Mr. Hyde" and Romans 7 : 14-25 : images of the moral duality of human nature
Author: L. Kreitzer
Publisher: *Literature and theology* 6(2), 125-144, ©1992

Sexual harassment isn't illegal in France, at least for now
Author: Unknown
Publisher: msnnow (Accessed May 5, 2012 from http://now.msn.com/now/0504-france-sexual-harassment.aspx)

Storey's curious compendium of practical and obscure skills : 214 things you can actually learn how to do
Editors: C. Madigan, S. Guare, and H. Fries
Publisher: North Adams, MA : Storey Publishing, ©2020

The denial of death
Author: Ernest Becker
Publisher: New York : The Free Press, ©1973

The future : six drivers of global change
Author: Al Gore
Publisher: New York : Random House, ©2013

The Jekyll and Hyde of emotional intelligence : emotion-regulation knowledge facilitates both prosocial and interpersonally deviant behavior
Authors: S. Côté, K. A. DeCelles, J. M. McCarthy, G. A. Van Kleef, and I. Hideg
Publisher: *Psychological science* 22(8) 1073–1080, ©2011

The quest for immortality : science at the frontiers of aging
Authors: Stuart Jay Olshansky and Bruce A. Carnes
Publisher: New York : W. W. Norton, ©2001

The teen's guide to social skills : practical advice for building empathy, self-esteem, & confidence
Author: Kate Fitzsimons
Publisher: Emeryville, CA : Rockridge Press, ©2021

The theology of the reformers and the anabaptists
Author: Dr. Jack L. Arnold
Publisher: *IIIM Magazine Online*, Volume 1, Number 12, ©1999. (Accessed October 27, 2022 from https://www.thirdmill.org/files/english/html/ch/ch.arnol d.rmt.11.html)

Through one lord only : theological interpretation of the meaning of διά in 1 cor 8,6
Author: Audrey Romanov
Publisher: *Biblica* 96(3) 391–415, ©2015. JSTOR, http://www.jstor.org/stable/43922738. (Accessed October 10, 2022)

This will change everything : ideas that will shape the future
Editor: John Brockman
Publisher: New York : Harper Perennial, ©2010

Under the rule of thumb : battered women and the administration of justice
Author: United States Commission on Civil Rights
Publisher: Washington, D.C. : The Commission, ©1982

I've got my talents, I've got my brains, I've got my love, I've got my passion, and I've got Christ... and a college degree at this point would be a very insignificant addition to that list. Also, I don't respect anyone with a college degree at all because I've seen how easy it is to get one, how little actual thought is involved, etc. Basically the only reason to get a college degree in 1992 is to make more money. And I don't want more money; less if possible. "And I believe you can do anything if you can love"--Rich Mullins, singer. That's not wishful thinking, that's what I believe almost more than anything in this earthly realm.

Life isn't too bad when you stop and look at the good things. ARRGGHH!!! Well, you can believe that if you want, and it's true that we must appreciate the good things-- definitely--but don't try and waylay the constant horrors of hatred, starvation, crime, abuse, perversion, etc. Bonhoeffer tried to express the sense in which we need to give up anxiety about "the morrow" without simultaneously abandoning ourselves to frivolously, resignedly, neglectfully living only for the moment. We need to plan and prepare, for ourselves and for future generations, but we also need to be wise and brave and cognizant of the fact that every single hour of every single day could potentially be the last in the land of the living for each one of us.

Be ready to live for many, many years if that is what happens, but be ready to die, and <u>live every day as if it were your last</u>. I like that a lot. I find it fairly easy to build this fire of passion within me when I think of the 40,000 young starving children for which this <u>will</u> be their last day on planet Earth. But I'm ready to keep serving and striving for another 70 years if that's what happens. (Actually, I must admit that

I'm not really willing to live that long. I really do see myself being killed, by someone who hates goodness, if I maintain my present passions and beliefs... and I will maintain them; I will increase them!)

Here's a thought I had recently: the reason why "good" people like JFK and Martin Luther King, etc. get killed is because their enemies, the "bad" people are willing to kill them. The reason why "bad" people stay alive and stay in power is because their enemies/opponents, the "good" people, are not willing to kill them. Does that make sense?

Please provide an accurate, online review of your opinion of this book if possible. (Thanks, if you have.)

Unfreeze * Change the World * Refreeze

Have you completed all of the 48 online surveys? (Thanks, if you have.)

Get jothed: https://youtu.be/MWVRXP0KtFY